The Enchanted Cross-Stitch

This book is dedicated to all of those who love cross-stitch.

Copyright © Christine Holly, 2024
All rights reserved. No part of this book may be reproduced or written in any manner without written permission of the copyright owner.
ISBN: 9798884349841

The Enchanted Cross-Stitch

by Christine Holly

1

Carol Crane paused her needlework to assess her progress, and to give her fingers and eyes a rest. She released a heavy sigh as she looked over her latest cross-stitch. Was the Aida evenly stretched? It was. Were her stitches uniform, neat, and free of knots? They were—for the most part. Something was not right. Perhaps it wasn't the right pattern. Carol wished she hadn't chosen this one. After all, she was considering entering this cross-stitch in next year's competition at the spring craft fair. She had chosen this pattern at Crafty Business, the craft store where she worked part-time, and Irene let her have it at a discount. The pattern displayed fresh-looking flowers in a vase. It would be a perfect gift for anyone, but if it happened to win in the competition, even third place, why then Carol would surely keep it and hang it on the wall with the third-place ribbon attached. Previously she had never won an award, but her hopes were high.

Carol regarded her work. Was it the thread, she thought? The colors appeared duller than shown on the package. She wished she had been able to buy a high-end thread, but she did not have unlimited funds. She was already working two jobs, albeit they were both minimum-wage jobs. Maybe Carol could request more hours. More hours. More hours for jobs she did not even like.

Then Carol saw it. She had made a mistake and would have to take out some stitches. Carol hated the tediousness of having to remove stitches. She considered leaving it, but you don't enter a noticeably flawed cross-stitch in a competition. She began to remove the stitches.

Carol knew she had bigger problems than taking out some stitches.

Gary said that because of the divorce, there would be a good number of changes in both their lives. One of those changes would be that they would have to sell the house. Gary told her she could not afford to keep it on her income. The house would be sold, and Carol would have to find somewhere else to live.

She could barely believe how quickly time had passed since they agreed to a divorce. Gary was already seeing someone else—Monica. Monica was... no, she did not know what type of person Monica was since they had never met. Carol was surprised that she was replaced so quickly. Gary seemed to be moving on in life without so much as a hiccup. Her mind went back to her pregnancy. They were both so very happy when they learned they were having a baby. Then the miscarriage. The depression. The tension between them. Carol did not feel appreciated. Is that all she was to him, a baby-maker? To be honest, she felt like a failure. So many failures in her life. She never finished college, never had a career, and then she failed at baby-making. So many women could do it. Why couldn't she? Now a failed marriage. No husband and no prospects. She was not ready for another relationship anyway. They seemed like a lot of work and lately, Carol just felt tired.

Gary said he would stop by next week, and that it was past time they started to settle things.

Carol was so certain about it when she asked for a divorce, now she wasn't so sure.

Her eyes went back to her cross-stitch. It was good, but it wasn't great, it wasn't flawless—like Tina's. Tina's cross-stitches were always flawless, much like Tina herself. Perfect cross-stitch, perfect makeup, perfect marriage. Tina always reminded Carol of how much her own life, through lack of effort, lacked excellence.

Carol regarded her work again. Should she scrap it and start on something else? No, it was... good. The scene depicted a floral arrangement in a vase. In the bouquet were red spray roses, fuchsia carnations, yellow Asiatic lilies, pale peach roses, red hypericum, orange gerberas, and bronze daisy poms. The arrangement was accented with goldenrods scattered amongst the bouquet. A stout, cream-colored ceramic vase with Japanese letters held the bouquet. There were a lot of curves in the pattern, so it required a lot of fractional stitches, which she found a bit tiresome.

Carol had loved it the first time she saw the pattern—and yet… it lacked something. Her stitching appeared uneven—she was not consistent with her stitching. Some appeared too tight while others were too loose. In a few cases, her count was off. The cloth looked dull and dirty. Carol knew it would have to be washed and ironed before it was framed. She hoped all the stains would come out.

Carol blew out in frustration causing her lips to sputter. Her phone rang. She answered it. On the line was an overly positive familiar voice.

"Hello, Carol, it's Amanda. How are you?"

Carol rolled her eyes from pure reflex. "I'm good, Amanda. How are you?"

"I am terrific, thanks for asking. I am super excited about our get-together tomorrow. I'm hosting, you know."

"Yes, I know."

"And I just thought I would call to remind you. You know you did miss that one meeting, and I did not want you to miss this one."

"Yes, I missed *one* meeting," Carol emphasized *one*.

"I didn't want you to miss tomorrow. One o'clock. I'm hosting, you know."

"I know. Are you sending reminder calls to everyone?"

There was a pause.

"No. Do you think I should? I mean you are the only one who ever missed. Tina will never forget, but Margaret is older. Do you think Margaret might forget? Harriet is older than Margaret. Does Harriet sometimes strike you as being absentminded? Should I call Harriet and remind her?

"Sure, Amanda, why don't you call her right now," Carol said, hoping Amanda would hang up and call Harriet.

"Maybe I will," Amanda said with a hint of urgency. "Did I tell you what I'm serving? I'm preparing a cheese tray with five different types of cheese and three kinds of crackers. I'll be able to use that new cheese platter—you know, the one I bought at Target. I'm putting out a fruit tray with two kinds of dip; with cream cheese and one with yogurt."

"Will there be booze… um, I mean drinks?" Carol asked bluntly.

Amanda was somewhat taken aback. "Well, yes. I'm serving wine, both red and white, which I am certain will go excellent with the food. The white is a subtle Pinot Grigio, and the red is—"

"It doesn't matter," Carol said. "I'll drink whatever you serve. See you tomorrow." She ended the call with Amanda calling out, "One o'clock!"

The next day Carol packed up her cross-stitch and supplies in her craft case and drove to Amanda's house. Amanda lived in a house much like Carol's in a neighborhood much like Carol's—a three-bedroom ranch with small rooms and a small yard. As she pulled up in front of the house Carol looked at her watch which read 1:15. Not too bad. Amanda and Tim Simons lived in a nice house with flowers out front, a low hedge, and trimmed shrubs. The house looked like dozens of others in the area with little to distinguish it from any other. 1:15—Amanda was probably getting ready to call Carol's number for another reminder.

Carol grabbed her purse and craft case and walked up the drive and onto the short walk that led to the front door. Amanda appeared with her typical happy and open expression, almost as if she were surprised to see Carol on her porch. She ushered Carol in and embraced her like a long-lost friend. Carol wrapped her arms around Amanda the best she could, her hands laden as they were.

"So glad you could come!" Amanda said. "Come in. Everyone is already here."

Of course, they are, Carol thought to herself. Only she would dare be fifteen minutes late to a meeting.

Amanda led Carol to the living room. Amanda stopped and announced in her usual upbeat tone, "I feel the itch—the itch to stitch!"

This was how Amanda liked to start every meeting when the women got together to cross-stitch and talk the afternoon away. It was a bit of an outdated reference, but Amanda was a huge Tom Cruise fan, and besides, everyone was used to it, and would not have it any other way. Amanda thought it was very funny, and she laughed every time she said it.

Three women had been sitting in conversation but turned and stood up as Carol and Amamda entered. Carol put down her things and embraced each one going from the oldest to the youngest in turn.

Harriet was the senior of the group. She was in her late sixties but still spry enough. And though she had been cross-stitching for many years, her fingers were still nimble and her eyes clear. She could keep up with the younger women and her cross-stitching was very nice. Harriet acted as the mother to the younger women of the group, having three grown children of her own, all of whom had married and moved away. Harriet seldom spoke of her husband, Cliff, who passed away almost fifteen years ago.

"Carol, dear, so good to see you," Harriet said, as they embraced, and Carol lightly kissed the woman's cheek. Harriet always used Gloria Vanderbilt Eau De Toilette Spray.

Next was Margaret, who did not appear openly friendly but was reliable and could be friendly if the mood suited her. Margaret was about fifty. She had no children and never married. She was reticent in talking about herself including her past. None of the others, including Carol, had the nerve to ask her openly for any personal details about herself. Sometimes Carol, Amanda, and Tina speculated that Margaret was a lesbian. It did not matter much to them, of course, but they liked to talk about it. Margaret never used scent.

Next came Tina. Carol had a secret resentment for Tina. The woman had an ego that made Carol cringe. Tina was the only one to ever wear a dress or a skirt to these cross-stitch meetings. Her hair and makeup were perfect. Who gets made up to come to one of these, Carol wondered. Tina did smell good, though.

Tina smiled and leaned into Carol giving her an air kiss so as not to disturb her makeup.

The women took their seats. "Where is the wine?" Carol asked.

Amanda frowned. "Oh, I won't put it out until later."

"Great," Carol said, managing to sound excited and disappointed at the same time.

Carol unpacked some of her supplies. She unzipped her case and took out the frame holding her cross-stitch.

"And how is your stitch coming along, my dear?" Harriet asked Carol.

Carol rose and carried her work over to Harriet. The older woman adjusted her glasses and gave Carol's work a quick assessment.

"It seems to be coming along fine. Yes, very fine."

"Thanks."

"Let us have a look," Margaret said. "Oh, yes. Very nice."

Wow! It was somewhat special getting even a mild compliment from Margaret who seldom commented on anyone's work.

Amanda and Tina came over to put in their two cents.

"I like it," Amanda said with just enough enthusiasm.

"Why, Amanda, sweetie," Tina said. "Don't you recognize that pattern? I did the same one a few years ago. I showed it to you."

Carol's heart sank.

"Oh, yes, I remember it now," Amanda said. Her enthusiasm slowly escaped her like a balloon deflating.

"Didn't I ever show you my Flowers in a Vase?" Tina asked Carol, who detected something condescending in her tone.

"No. I don't believe so."

"Next time you are over to my house, remind me and I will show you. Come over and see what I am working on," Tina said, tapping Carol's arm as if to say, *Leave that, and come and see some good cross-stitch.*

Carol rested her plastic clip frame on her chair and followed Tina to her work. It was stretched in a wooden scroll frame. Tina held it up as if it were already a prize winner.

Carol fought against the urge to gasp. It was Madonna and Child reminiscent of paintings done in the Renaissance period. It was not complete, of course, but Carol could see the incredible beauty of it. Mary's eyes alone were almost hypnotic, and the expression captured on her face fought for the joy of motherhood and the incredible sadness she would experience during Christ's passion. The baby Jesus perfectly embodied the innocence of childhood and the overwhelming knowledge of what was to come.

"What is that—Evenweave?" Carol asked.

"Jobelan—32 count," Tina said haughtily. "I just love the look and feel of it. It gives the work a richness. I wouldn't use anything else."

"Lovely," Carol said.

When it appeared as if Carol could not absorb any more of its beauty, Tina gave the frame a quick flip to reveal the back. The backs of some cross-stitches, Carol concluded, were not very neat, with loose threads and looking a bit of a mess. But Tina's was as neat, orderly, and clean on the back as the front. There was no other reason to show Carol the back of the work other than to say, *The back of my work looks better than the front of yours.*

"Just beautiful," was all Carol could say.

The afternoon went by as it always did. In between stitches was the latest gossip, stories retold, and plans for future meetings.

Carol was starting to feel a bit edgy.

"Is it time for the wine?" she asked.

Amanda looked at the clock on the wall and checked it against her watch.

"I was going to put out the wine with the cheese and crackers," Amanda said.

"Then put out the cheese and crackers and serve it with wine," Carol said.

"It's too early, isn't it?" Amanda said making a face like it was an unforgivable faux pas. "Isn't it too early to put out the food? What do you think, Tina? Should I put the food out?"

Tina shrugged. "Sure, put it out."

"I'll put it out," Amanda said happily.

The food and drink break allowed Carol to see everyone's progress. Amanda was working on a small cross-stitch in a hoop frame of a cat. There must have been about thirty colors. It was nice, and Amanda said it was the kind of cat she would have if she weren't allergic.

Margaret was working on the interior of an old-fashioned kitchen. It was a good size project, about a foot square. A woman was taking pies out of an oven. There was an open window where a pie sat on the sill cooling. Other pies sat on a table. Above the scene were the words, *Happiness is a Freshly Baked Pie.*

Harriet's cross-stitch was a very lovely piece. A winged angel close-up and in profile. There was beautiful detail in the wings and robe. Harriet was using silver thread to accent the wings. She planned on adding a few small pearl-like studs as well. Atop the piece were the words, *God Bless.*

The wine ran out before the food, but that was mainly due to Carol who had more than her share.

"Carol, have you heard from Gary?" Tina asked. It was a bit of an indelicate question, and the others went silent. "What is the name of his new girlfriend?"

Leave it to Tina, Carol thought and wished there had been one glass of wine left. She tried to look as if the question did not bother her.

"Her name is Monica. Gary and I plan to meet very soon

to begin to settle matters. We may have to sell the house." For some reason, Carol refrained from saying the house had to be sold. She was trying to hang on to the house as long as possible.

"Oh, Carol dear, that is a shame," Harriet said.

"What kind of settlement are you getting from Gary?" Tina asked.

Tina could be tactless when she wished to be, and Carol fought against the urge to tell Tina that it was none of her business.

"It is too early to know about that," Carol said. "Nothing has been settled."

"What does your lawyer say?" Tina asked.

Harriet decided to step in.

"Carol, if this is too sensitive, you don't have to talk about it," she said sympathetically. "We all understand how difficult this must be for you."

"Thank you, Harriet," Carol said. "You're right, it is difficult to talk about, but I consider every woman here my friend, and if you can't turn to your friends during times of trouble, who can you turn to?"

This touched everyone in the room, and they all respected Carol more for it.

"To be honest, I did not want this," Carol said. "It wasn't part of a plan, and I did not see this coming. Things just seemed to fall apart faster than we could put them back together. I don't blame Gary for what happened. I don't blame myself. I wish we had tried harder, but sometimes you just get so tired of trying, and before you know it, your life is in pieces."

Her eyes began to water, and everyone could see the sheer honesty that Carol was displaying. Though her statement was not entirely true it certainly was touching and one that garnered sympathy.

Harriet went over to Carol with her arms out. Carol stood and the two women embraced. This, of course, led to the other women following suit.

By 4:30 Amanda announced it was probably a good idea for everyone to start packing up.

"Tim will be home soon, and he doesn't like it when you all are here," Amanda said, trying to be lighthearted about it. "If we can all get our things together, that would be great." She paused raising a loose fist to her mouth. It looked as if she was on the verge of tears.

Harriet stepped forward and gently took Amanda by the shoulders. "Amanda, honey, what is it? What is the matter?"

Amanda choked back sobs. "Things are not too good between Tim and me. I think he is having an affair."

There sounded a collective sigh from the group, and everyone moved in closer. There came forth words and sounds of comfort and sympathy. The words came from everyone but Carol. She carefully watched Amanda who seemed to soak it all in, privately reveling in the attention. Carol knew Amanda could be a bit of a drama queen, an attention seeker, a crisis junkie. Amanda saw how Carol was the center of attention at this meeting and felt jealous. Carol suspected Amanda of actually making up the story, or at least exaggerating the story just for attention.

They all sat back down again in the living room and continued to comfort Amanda, who did not give clear details of the situation. At one point she said it was only a suspicion. Margaret and Carol cleaned up. They put the glasses and the plates in the sink and submerged them in hot soapy water. They put away what food remained in the refrigerator and got rid of the empty wine bottles.

When Tim drove up, Amanda asked everyone not to say a word, which helped confirm Carol's suspicion that some if not all of Amanda's story was concocted.

The four women hugged and said goodbye to Amanda, and all glared at Tim as they walked out. Before getting in their cars, Tina reminded everyone that the next get-together would be at her house.

On the drive home, Carol did not think of Amanda's sad situation, for she had already made up her mind that the story was not entirely true. No, Carol thought about the next meeting at Tina's house and how she would have to endure Tina's perfect cross-stitch, her perfect house, her perfect husband, and her perfect life. And of course, Tina had the best cross-stitch materials. She had hundreds and hundreds of thread colors and different types of thread: Perle, cotton, Marlitt, and even Metallic. When it came to fabrics, no one in the group knew more about linen, Hardanger, and fancy weaves. Tina had all the equipment any stitcher would ever need: compass cutter, craft knife, easy turn, hole punch, bodkins, and even vanishing ink pens.

Carol gripped the steering wheel harder when she recalled how Tina had not only refrained from giving Carol's cross-stitch any praise, but she got in a subtle jibe. *Oh, she did that cross-stitch years ago! When you come to my house, I will show you.* I'd like to show her, Carol thought.

That was Carol's secret ambition—to show up Tina. To prove she was good at something, and not a failure.

When she arrived home, she started to search through her forgotten stash of patterns she had bought with the honest intention of completing them one day but ended up tucked away in a cupboard. She referred to this stash as her SINS—Stuff I'll Never Stitch. Carol pulled out bags of patterns, some she remembered exactly where and when she purchased them, some she did not remember buying at all. After going through them all, she did not find any that would seem to do the trick. None of them were prize-winners. I guess these will remain my SINS, she thought.

Next, she went through her cross-stitch magazines. She had dozens of them. When she exhausted her collection of magazines, she went online looking and looking and looking.

She did not know why, but none of the patterns she saw caught her eye.

Carol was tired. She needed to go to bed. She had to go to work tomorrow. After work, she would hit all the craft stores she knew. She was determined to find a pattern that would impress Tina and prove she was a good cross-stitcher.

2

The town of Bedford, like all the towns in New Hampshire, is a historic town and very scenic. It is close to Manchester, and only fifty miles from Boston, but still was able to maintain that small-town feel. Like most New England towns, Bedford concerned itself with the safety of its citizens, community activities, housing, neighborhood advancements, and the quality of life for the community.

In Bedford, one could buy a coffee at one of the many coffee shops and enjoy it in one of Bedford's many scenic and relaxing parks. You could even take your coffee and sit by the shore of the mighty Merrimack as it flowed south and into Massachusetts.

There were over twenty craft stores in the area and Carol had visited every one of them. One of her jobs was working part-time at Crafty Business in Bedford. It was not your high-end craft store, but Carol did get a discount on her supplies.

The woman who owned and ran Crafty Business was Irene Weston. That day when Carol went to work, she approached Irene to explain to her that she needed a cross-stitch pattern for the next Spring Craft Fair. It had to be something extraordinary, something eye-catching, something that would get her one of the top three ribbons.

Irene Weston was about fifty and had owned Crafty Business for almost twenty years. She looked at Carol sympathetically over her glasses. She turned from Carol, removed her glasses, and let them dangle from the light chain around her neck.

"Carol, honey, I am going to be honest with you," Irene began. "I think you might be aiming too high at winning a place at the craft fair."

"What do you mean?"

"Carol, I have seen your work. It's good, but not good enough to win a ribbon. I have been in this line for some time. I have seen award winners. I know what it takes. You simply do not have what it takes. I'm sorry."

Carol stood dumb and numb. She could not move. She could not speak. Her gorge rose in her throat, and she felt as if someone was choking her. Tears welled in her eyes. Carol felt any enthusiasm she had about cross-stitching and winning a ribbon at the craft fair, leaving her body like some weird type of exorcism. Empty—that is how it felt when Irene said this to her.

Without a word, Carol turned and went about her work taking inventory, stocking the shelves, and answering the telephone.

The rest of the workday she moved about like an automaton. At the end of the day, she gave Irene a curt goodbye and left the store. Carol sat in her car staring over the steering wheel. Was Irene right? Should she simply give up on this crazy idea of creating an award-winning cross-stitch? Carol had been cross-stitching for about ten years. She had always enjoyed it. The completion of a pattern had always given her joy. It was an accomplishment, and she believed she was good at it. People had said so. What people? Who, Amanda, Margaret, and Harriet? They were just being nice. It's good, they would say, but Carol would sometimes hear a hesitancy in their words, a reluctance to be completely honest. Tina may have been the most honest by not praising Carol's work.

She looked down at her hands that rested in her lap. She moved her fingers. They worked. They were nimble enough. But it would take more than that to achieve her goal. To hell with Irene. Carol was determined to find that one special pattern that would change everything. What if it didn't exist? No, it did, and she was determined to find it.

Carol lost track of the craft stores she visited. All of them she had been in previously. After several stores, she noticed that they all seemed to smell the same. They all appeared to have the same patterns. Large or small, pricey, or reasonable, none of them had what she wanted. The thought struck her that perhaps she would have better luck if she went somewhere new. She drove south down the 101.

Soon Carol arrived in the small town of Amherst. She stayed away from the franchises and the stores that appeared to be like all the others. After driving around town and making a few inquiries Carol found a craft store outside of town.

A sign out front read Amherst Craft Supplies. It was run by a husband and wife by the name of Harper. There was only one other customer in the store, so Carol was able to have the attention of both Harpers who were interested in helping her. Carol explained to the Harpers what she was looking for, and they did their best to accommodate her, but like all the other places they came up short of her expectations. She thanked them and left the store.

Carol was sitting in her car wondering if she should go home. It was getting late, and she was tired of craft stores, tired of looking at the same boring patterns, and tired of being disappointed.

A knock on her window made her jump. So startled was she that Carol let out a short cry and clutched at her heart, and then tried to bring her breathing down to normal. Another knock, this one sounded softer, caused Carol to turn slowly to her left. A woman stood peering at her. She was older than Carol, perhaps in her fifties, wearing thick glasses, plainly dressed, with a kerchief on her head, and looked a bit familiar. Of course, thought Carol, this woman was in Amherst Craft Supplies. The woman made a gesture for Carol to roll down her window. Carol hesitated. She did not know why she did. Maybe because it was night, the parking lot was dark, and this woman was a stranger. The woman motioned again. Carol brought the window down about four inches.

"Yes?"

"I am sorry to bother you, dear, but I could not help but overhear your conversation in the supply store."

"Yes?"

"I understand you are looking for a cross-stitch pattern... something different... something special."

"Yes, I am."

"I happen to know a craft store. It's a little out of the way, but they specialize in unique crafts and materials. I believe you will find what you are looking for there."

"Thank you. What is the name of this store?"

"Malum Crafts."

"Where is it located?"

"Do you have a pencil and paper so you can write down the directions?"

"Can you just give me the address so I can put it on my phone? I have GPS."

"Sorry, I don't know the address, but I can give you directions."

The woman's directions were somewhat confusing, as she contradicted herself and sounded uncertain about landmarks and roads. Carol wrote down the directions as best she could, and then thanked her. She watched the woman smile and walk away. Carol watched her fade into the darkness and realized she hadn't even gotten the woman's name. She tapped the paper on which she wrote down the directions, then looked at her watch. What were the odds that she could find the place and that it would be open when she got there?

Carol chose to take a chance.

She drove south to Milford, then headed west passed Wilton, and turned off the main road. There were a few turns after that, and it looked as if she were headed into a heavily wooded area. Carol studied the directions to be certain she hadn't made a mistake. She was certain she had followed them correctly. She was just as certain she was lost. There were no lights anywhere. She had not seen a house for miles. Pulling the car onto the shoulder of the road, she thought about what she should do.

Carol decided the next road she came to she would turn around and backtrack. A road appeared on her left and she slowed down and turned onto it. She was about to put the car in reverse when her headlights lit up something.

"Well, I'll be damned," she whispered.

She wasn't on a road at all. It was a short driveway. At the end of the driveway was a wooden building with a wooden sign out front. Malum Crafts, it read. A dim light flickered over the porch, but it looked like the store was closed. It did not look as if there was a light on in the place. Carol got out of the car and approached the small, low porch. The closer she came the more it looked as if there was a light inside. She tried the doorknob. It turned. She pushed in the door. It opened. The door had one of those old-fashioned brass shopkeeper bells that rang when the door opened. The bell startled her a bit. Carol closed the door and stood still, looking around. The store appeared empty. She let out a low *hello*. There was no response. She raised her voice and tried again. Still, no response.

Carol looked about. It looked like an old shop that hadn't changed in sixty years. Everything was built with wooden boards. The floor creaked when you walked on it, the ceiling was low, and the walls were practically covered with crafts, pictures, memory boxes, frames, and garden signs. There was knitting wool and crochet yarn of every color. Hanging in rows were strings of beads. There were materials and threads, kits, and paints. There were shelves, racks, and cubby holes.

The store was longer than it appeared outside. It was very deceptive. Carol looked down the rows and got dizzy. The store did not have the typical odor that the other stores had. This was definitely a different type of odor. What was that smell? Incense? Burning hemp? Marijuana?

Carol swore she saw someone, or something move at the far end of the store. What was that?

She let out another hello.

"Yes, may I help you?"

The voice seemed to come out of nowhere. Carol started. She looked over at the checkout counter near the door and a woman stood behind the counter. Carol was certain the woman was not there when she walked in. She surely would have noticed.

The woman was tall and very thin. She looked sickly. The woman wore no makeup and her clothes looked handmade and put together with pieces of discarded cloth. She overdid it with the jewelry, though. She wore an abundance of rings, necklaces, earrings, and bracelets, all silver. Her long and frizzy hair was completely grey, though she did not appear old. Carol could not tell the woman's age. It appeared to fluctuate depending on the angle and point of view. She had tired eyes, a wide flat mouth, and pale skin.

"May I help you with something?" the woman repeated. Her voice sounded calm, almost detached. Carol detected a bit of an accent. Not the East Coast kind of accent, but something European perhaps. Maybe the woman was a Francophone from Quebec. Her lips and jaw moved little when she spoke.

"I wasn't even certain you were open," Carol said. "I thought I was lost, then…. I saw a light… uhm… the door was open… so I came in. Do you own this store?"

The woman nodded. "I run it. Are you looking for something… unique?"

"Why, yes, I am."

The woman continued to stare at Carol with a deadpan expression.

"Do you have any cross-stitch patterns?"

The woman nodded slowly.

"I am looking for something different… eye-catching. I need something… award-winning. Might you have something like that?"

The woman came out from behind the counter. She wore a pinkish, floor-length skirt. Carol could not decide on what kind of material it was. The woman said nothing, nor did she beckon Carol in any way, but Carol followed her to the back of the store. The woman stopped and looked at Carol, who in turn looked about expectantly. The woman gestured toward the wall. Carol followed her gesture with her eyes.

Here the ceiling rose high, and there, high up on the wall were framed works of cross-stitch, but they were like no cross-stitch she had seen. Each one was distinct. One was the profile of a beautiful young woman whose long blond hair seemed to cascade off the Aida cloth. The young woman wore a silk gown that appeared to shimmer, and in her hair were small flowers. Her face was profile and her expression bespoke beauty, innocence, and wonder.

Another cross-stitch depicted a log cabin in the woods surrounded by snow-laden fir trees. Smoke rose from the chimney of the cabin and the smoke appeared to roll and move until it broke off. Almost hidden in the darkness of the woods, yellow eyes glowed, winking on and off. A shadow moved behind the opaque window of the cabin.

Yet another was a cross-stitch of a Persian rug. The main color of the rug was vibrant blood-red, and within the red were intricate patterns and designs in green and gold. In the weave were diamond shapes of soft beige and grey. The pattern of the rug was an intricate maze of designs leading the observer's eyes to the center and then out again to the very fringes of the rug, and then inward again. It was almost dizzying.

Each of the cross-stitch had the stitcher's initials stitched in the lower right-hand corner of the work.

"They are wonderful," Carol said, under her breath. "They all must be 32-count linen."

"40-count."

"Forty?" Carol uttered. "I've never heard of 40-count."

"It is a custom-made linen."

"Do you have any of these patterns?" Carol said, indicating the framed works on the wall.

"These are all one-of-a-kind."

"One-of-a-kind? I don't understand."

"You will never see these anywhere else."

Carol shook her head, confused.

"They are one-of-a-kind," the woman reiterated.

"They must be very expensive."

"They are."

"How would I get one."

"We carry them. We are the only ones who do."

Carol thought this very peculiar, still, she asked, "Do you have any in store or do you have to order them?"

"I have one you might be interested in."

"One. May I see it?"

The woman led Carol back to the checkout counter. She went behind it, reached down, and placed a large box on the counter. At first, Carol thought it looked like a jigsaw puzzle box. There on the lid was the image of the cross-stitch. The image was a scene from a small town in the late 19th century. In the very center was a covered bandstand. It resembled an octagonal gazebo. Several characters, men, women, and children in old-style dress were on the streets. There were shops and other buildings. There was a horse and buggy. A sign on the bandstand held the name of the town—Smith Falls.

Carol thought it was very quaint, very picturesque. The entire scene spoke of a slower, gentler time. The longer she looked at the scene the more she wanted it.

"How much is it?'

"This kit comes with all the floss. It is the very best floss, made specially for this project. This thread does not run or fade—ever. It comes with 40-count linen, needle, and a wooden frame. There are directions, and they must be followed to the letter."

"Directions?"

"This is not just any cross-stitch that you find at any craft store. This is one-of-a-kind. This is for someone looking for something special, something unique. This would guarantee anyone a blue ribbon."

Carol was not certain if it was the odor of this place or the woman's droning voice, but she felt her head spin as if she caught a sudden case of vertigo.

"I feel like you're setting me up for a very big number," Carol said. "For the last time, how much is it?"

The woman gave a brief shake of her head. "For you, it's free."

"Free? What do you mean free? You just said how special it is, finest floss and all that."

"I know what I said. For you, it's free. But there are stipulations."

"Oh, here it comes."

"You must use only the material that is in this kit. As I stated, you must follow the directions. You cannot share any of the material in the box with anyone, not even that pattern."

"That does not make much sense," Carol said, skeptically.

"You don't have to take it. Maybe you can find something at Michaels."

Carol looked at the scene on the box and thought of the framed cross-stitch she had just seen hanging on the wall. She had never seen anything like them. This cross-stitch could guarantee Carol a 1st place ribbon."

"I'll take it," she said.

The woman behind the counter cocked her head and regarded Carol closely.

"Are you certain this is what you want?"

The woman's look and question were disconcerting.

"Yes, I'm certain."

The woman picked up the box and proffered it to Carol, who received it carefully.

"Everything I need is in here?" Carol asked.

"Everything you need is in that box."

"So, it's a kit. Everything included."

The woman did not respond with a nod or a word. She simply looked at Carol—or stared at her, was more accurate. It was a bit of an unnerving stare.

"Thank you," Carol said. "I'm sure to come back."

The woman said nothing but watched Carol as she walked out of the shop. The bell rang again. Even the bell sounded a bit off.

Once out the door, she stood on the wooden stoop. The light above her head flickered, then went out. She was left in the darkness. Carol could barely see her car in the night. She felt relieved when she was inside. If this were a movie, the car would not start, she thought to herself. The car started. She retraced her journey and went home. The familiar streets of Bedford felt reassuring.

3

When she woke in the morning Carol thought the trip to Malum Crafts was a dream and not a good dream. It was a bit creepy, and the experience left her feeling uneasy. She made herself a coffee and looked at the box she had left on the kitchen table last night when she arrived home. It was late when she got home and was too tired to even open the box. It had sat next to her on the ride home and she found herself taking sidelong glances at it, almost as if expecting it to disappear. How did she come to have this, she wondered. She kept replaying the experience of the creepy craft store and the even creepier craft lady in her head. But the more she tried to remember, the more confused she became about what happened and what was said. By the time she arrived home she felt exhausted, so leaving the box on the table she went directly to bed.

Carol drank her coffee and stared at the box. Why did she feel reluctant to open it? Was it because once it was open, she could never get the genie back in the bottle? That sounded ridiculous. What did she have to fear?

Picking up the box Carol walked into the living room, sat in the center of the couch, and set the box on the coffee table before her. She looked over the scene on the lid. Smith Falls. It looked like a lovely little town. She opened the box, removed its contents one by one, and took inventory. Right on top were the floss skeins, twenty-three of them. The woman at the craft store was not exaggerating, there was something very special about the floss. Carol could tell just by fingering it. She held out a few strands. The floss appeared to shimmer in the light and the colors were vibrant.

Next, she took out the 40-count linen. Carol had never seen linen like this. Like the floss, the linen had a different feel. The cloth had both a softness and a texture that held a distinct durability beyond any other linen she had seen.

There was a long, thin needle, and like all cross-stitch needles, it had a long eye and a blunt tip. It looked thin and delicate. Carol hoped it wouldn't break.

Carol took out the four pieces of wood for the frame.

Finally, at the bottom of the box was the pattern. She took it out and unfolded it as it was three times the size to easily see the count. On the back of the pattern was a list of instructions. The first instruction was that every instruction was to be followed exactly. The second instruction was that the cross-stitch was not to be passed on to anyone before, during, or after its completion. None of the materials, not the floss, nor the linen, nor the pattern, nor even the needle was to be shared with anyone. The remainder of the instructions had to do with the mechanics of the cross-stitch.

Step One; assemble the frame.

Carol found this quite simple as it required no tools.

Step Two; secure linen inside the frame provided.

This too was quite easy and soon she had the linen secured and stretched neat and even within the frame.

There were even instructions on which floss (all of them numbered) to begin with. It specified how many strands to use, how to thread it, and what length of floss to use.

Now, some people might begin their cross-stitch in the middle, some may begin at the edge or a corner. Some reserve the right to start wherever they wish. The instructions specified that this cross-stitch was to begin in the middle which was marked by a brown spot. That spot was the peak of the outdoor bandstand.

Carol cut her floss to length and separated two strands. She threaded her needle and sat poised to make her first stitch. Why was she so hesitant? It was as if she were ready to embark upon a new adventure. But that was what a project was, wasn't it? To create something new and beautiful that was not there before. To be able to prove she was good at something.

From the rear, Carol stuck her needle in the center and pulled the floss through while holding the end of the floss between her forefinger and thumb. She made her first stitch as directed in the instructions, then two more stitches before she anchored the end of the floss in the rear. Carol looked at the first few stitches. She wanted to remember them.

Carol made her fourth stitch, then her fifth. She was well on her way, each stitch became easier as she went, despite the 40-count. Occasionally she would stop to check if her floss was twisting, but it never did.

So engrossed in her work, Carol did not seem to hear her phone. In the back of her mind, she wondered what the noise was, and finally, she realized. Carol was reluctant to put down her cross-stitch, but the phone would not stop ringing. Laying aside her work, she answered her phone. It was Irene Weston, at Crafty Business.

"Hello."

"Carol, are you coming in today? You were supposed to be here at 11:00."

Carol looked at the clock on the wall. It was a little after noon. Carol was tempted to lie and say she was sick, but she needed the money, and she did not want to leave Irene shorthanded. The cross-stitch would be here when she returned from work.

"I'm leaving for work right now," Carol said and hung up.

Despite Irene giving her the cold shoulder and a nasty glance when she finally arrived at work, Carol felt energized and somewhat delighted. She had garnered such joy from the new cross-stitch and could not wait to get back to it, finding it difficult to think of anything else. Despite wishing to get home to her cross-stitch, she told Irene she would stay longer and make up for her lost time.

For the next few days, Carol worked on her cross-stitch. Every day she assessed her work and progress. It was coming along wonderfully. She had completed the bandstand and was amazed at how splendid it looked. It had to be the linen and the floss, Carol decided. Somehow the two materials gave the image not only depth but a stark realism, more like a clear photograph, rather than a cross-stitch.

Day by day the cross-stitch grew and expanded. Little by little, stitch by stitch, Smith Falls became more real to Carol, and she often secretly thought that Smith Falls was a place she would like to visit.

When she was not fantasizing about Smith Falls, Carol could see how her skills were improving. Her cross-stitching looked practically flawless. Every stitch appeared to blend into the others, more of an endless stream rather than individual stitches. The colors were vibrant, the lines smooth, not staggered. Here was work she could be proud of. Here was work that could win her a blue ribbon.

A knock at the door surprised her. Carol put down her cross-stitch, walked across to the window, and saw Gary's car out front. She cast a glance in the mirror and saw she looked like a mess. Doing what she could, Carol went to the door and opened it with a smile.

Wow! She thought to herself. Gary looked great. Healthy and handsome and neatly dressed. His shoes and clothes looked new. Monica must have bought them for him. Carol recalled how Gary hated to shop for clothes.

"Hello, Gary."

"Hello."

Carol stood there staring at him. He looked happy. Happier than he'd been for a while. Dozens of emotions and memories passed through her mind. She remembered how he looked when they first started dating. He looked practically the same. He looked fit. He was running again, she supposed.

"I didn't expect you today," she said.

"We talked last week and decided on today."

"Oh, was it today?" Carol realized she was staring. "Oh… come on in."

Gary stepped into the living room and looked around. Everything was exactly how it had been months ago when he left.

"How have you been?" she asked.

"Good. And you?"

"Good."

This was certainly awkward, Carol thought.

"You look good," she said.

"Thanks."

Gary did not return the compliment.

"Sit down. Would you like something to drink?"

"No, I'm good."

They both sat down, acutely aware of the awkwardness of the situation.

"How have you been?" Carol asked.

"You asked me that."

"Oh, yeah," Carol said. "How's work?"

"Work is good. I got a promotion."

"Great."

"Not much of a raise, but it's something. Still at the craft store?"

"Yes, and I also work part-time at the Golden Griddle."

"That's good."

"Speaking of crafts, I want to show you my latest cross-stitch," Carol said with a hint of excitement. She reached over and picked up her work.

"You're still doing those?"

"Yes, but this one is completely different. It's a new project, but you can see how different it is from others I've done—different from any I have ever seen." Carol held the work before him to look at.

"Wow. That is very nice. That is different."

Isn't it, though?" she said, holding it in front of her eyes. She never got tired of looking at it. It was almost hypnotic. She turned it back towards Gary with a wide, proud smile. "Isn't it lovely?"

"Yes, very lovely. Listen, Carol, I didn't come here to talk about your latest cross-stitch. There are a lot of things we need to settle."

"What things?"

Gary shook his head and raised his hands in frustration.

"This house, for one," he said. "You can't afford to keep it. We have to sell it."

"Why? Why can't I just live here?"

"Carol, it's not paid for. There's a mortgage which you cannot afford."

"Can't you pay it?"

"We're getting divorced, remember. I can't afford to pay for two mortgages."

"Two? Oh, yes, two mortgages."

"You can get a smaller place—someplace you can afford. You can rent. You could find a roommate. You have several options open to you."

He continued to talk but Carol failed to hear a word he said. She felt her life crumbling, like on YouTube when they showed a huge building being demolished with explosives and the entire structure collapsing in on itself in slow motion. Gary continued to prattle on.

The noise coming out of Gary stopped and he stood up. She had hardly heard a word he said. Carol looked up at him and focused.

"So, we'll get together again soon, and begin to settle things," Gary said.

Carol stood and Gary turned to the door and showed himself out. She continued to stand in the same spot after he pulled away in his car. She felt like crying, but the tears would not come.

She could not remember a time when she felt so lonely, so abandoned. Carol turned and looked at her cross-stitch sitting where she had left it on the sofa. For the first time since she started working on it, she had no desire to continue. Pouring herself a drink, she sat and drank and looked about the house. Memories came and went fleetingly through her mind. She and Gary had picked out this house together. They had such dreams about it. Their life together was in front of them, and the possibilities seemed endless. Every day they made plans for their future. Their lives held such certainty. Now, the house was so quiet, so empty. Her life was empty. Carol regarded the cross-stitch again. With her drink in her hand, she went over to her work, regarding it closely. The happiness she felt while working on it came back to her. She did feel happy when she worked on it. It was fulfilling. She had done cross-stitch for years, but somehow, she knew this one was different—almost life-changing. That is what she wanted—for her life to change.

Carol picked up the cross-stitch and sat with it at the end of the sofa where she had set up an OttLite. She began to cross-stitch.

The bandstand was complete, and she was happy to move on. There was a street lined with shops—a haberdashery next to a seamstress shop, there was a florist, a candy store, and a small art gallery with a framed picture of a young woman in the front window.

Carol continued to cross-stitch with no sense of the time. Time was unimportant to her while she worked on it. She was not aware hours had passed. Carol was barely aware that her eyes were growing heavy with sleep. She hoped to soon finish the young couple walking along the street. The man wore a high hat, grey with a brown band. He was dressed in a long coat. His companion wore an electric blue dress that reached the ground. A lovely bonnet adorned her head. The woman had blonde hair and fine features. The floss lent a life-like quality to the couple. They both looked young, and there was detail in their appearance.

Carol's fingers began to falter. She fought off fatigue. She wanted to complete the young couple. When I get them done, I'll stop and sleep, she thought to herself. I just need to get them done.

Her fingers moved almost mechanically but with purpose. Stitch after stitch. The instructions called for stitches to be done from left to right, then the cross from right to left. Almost there, she thought. If I get the couple done, I'll stop.

Finally, they were done, and they looked simply wonderful. There seemed to be an innocence about their faces and their attitude reflected that old-world manner and charm that appealed to Carol. It reminded her of a Jane Austin book she once read. Just a young couple taking a stroll in town on a sunny day, perhaps in Spring. How lucky they were to have one another. Did they love one another? Of course, they did. You could see it on their faces, the way she hooked his arm. He had brought up his other hand to lay upon hers. They were smiling.

Carol's eyes grew heavier. The young couple looked as if they were looking directly at her. They were smiling at her. They appeared to be closer. Closer. The couple looked as if they were about to say something to Carol.

4

Carol felt the sun on her face. It felt glorious. Never had sunshine felt so good, not even when she was a child and played outside with her friends during the summer, which at times seemed endless. Sunshine was an excellent source of vitamin D, she knew, and it felt as if she were getting an extreme boost of it now. Carol closed her eyes and turned her face to the sun. This was exactly what she needed. Her body told her so. She felt wonderful and energized. Her senses were alive. Hypersensitivity coursed through her and around her, causing her to be aware of her being—her heightened senses, heartbeat, and brain activity. She even seemed to be aware of the blood coursing through her veins.

She breathed in. Oh, what a breath! Never had she experienced an air of this quality. She felt it filling her lungs and she held it there for a time to retain the sensation and get its full effects. The oxygen content felt invigorating. Letting her breath out slowly, she immediately took in another. The sensation reminded her of getting high. It was life-giving, it was life-sustaining. A happiness she had never known flowed over and through her. She felt content just to stand here in the sun breathing in and out.

Eventually, Carol turned her face away from the sun and opened her eyes. A yellow glow blurred her vision, and she had to wait until her eyes cleared.

She saw that she was standing on a street corner. Across the street was a covered bandstand. She knew it. She knew it very well as if she had constructed it herself. It was raised and a few steps led to the wooden floor. It was octagonal in shape and flowerpots hung down between the posts. A wooden rail with decorative spindles ran about the circumference. The roof was conical and lined with cedar shake shingles. Upon the bandstand was a sign denoting the town—Smith Falls. Carol smiled. She smiled with genuine happiness. She was dreaming, her mind told her. This was all a dream. So enamored was she with her cross-stitch, that she was now seeing it in her dreams.

Looking about slowly, Carol saw buildings and streets. Nothing appeared to be moving. No, that was not quite right. In the distance, a horse-drawn buggy went by. Strangely, the clip-clop of the horse's hoofs was like a rhythm. Two children were playing with a ball and their bouts of laughter possessed a certain cadence and together with the horse's hoofs created a musical phrase. A breeze caressed her cheek like a loving touch. Carol turned and faced the breeze causing her to smile. The breeze rustled the leaves in a tree and the sound spoke to Carol in an unknown language that possessed intelligence and purpose. It was a message aimed at her heart and she wished she could decipher it.

Everything seemed alive and part of something splendiferous.

Carol turned to see a well-dressed handsome couple walking toward her. They were smiling at her. She knew their faces and those smiles.

The man was dressed in a tall grey hat with a brown band that perfectly matched his long frock coat and trousers. Beneath his coat, he wore a white linen shirt and wing collar. A four-in-hand tie was partly hidden by his waistcoat or vest.

His companion was shorter than him, her head coming up to his chin. She was dressed in a beautiful electric blue dress with a closed neckline. Her narrow sleeves flared out at her wrists. A matching cape hung from her shoulders. Her blonde hair was pulled back and piled atop her head. Atop that, a cute bonnet with ribbons sat precariously a bit to one side. Shielding her from the sun, the woman held an open parasol above her head. The parasol was dove-grey in color with a short fringe and an ivory tip. The woman's gloves matched her parasol.

As Carol and the couple approach one another, Carol sees that she too carries a parasol. Hers was white silk. She opened it and held it aloft.

"Good day," the man said in a friendly tone, tipping his hat.

"Good day, Caroline," his companion said, smiling.

"Good day," Carol replied, automatically. "I am afraid you have the advantage of me."

"I do beg your pardon," the man said, sincerely. "My name is Robert C. Crawford." He turned to the young woman. "This is my fiancé, Miss Penelope Hope."

"It is a pleasure to meet you both," Carol said.

"Is it not a lovely day?" Miss Hope said, casting a glance at the sky.

"It surely is," said he. "How are you, Caroline?"

"I am very well, thank you."

"Are you enjoying your walk?" the woman asked her.

"Yes. It is quite splendid."

"Would you care to join us?" Miss Hope offered.

"Why, yes I would, if I would not be intruding."

"No, not at all."

Robert Crawford offered Carol his free arm, and she took it.

"Now I feel perfectly balanced," he said. "A lovely woman on each side."

They all laughed at this and walked down the street lined with shops.

They stopped briefly before a haberdashery. In the window, Carol saw her reflection and saw what she was wearing.

It was a lovely day dress of light blue with beaded stripes. Her cuffs and hem were trimmed in bands of burnt gold. It was form-fitting, long-waisted, with a bone bodice that reached below her hips. The neckline was square-cut and had a modest bustle behind along with a short train. Carol wore ivory gloves trimmed with small pearl buttons.

Carol touched her hair which was pulled back and hung down past her neck in two ringlets. Her hat was modest but most becoming.

The trio moved on to a florist shop. They went inside and the man purchased a small bouquet for his female companions. Carol smelled the flowers and was surprised at how fragrant they smelled. The colors of the flowers were deep and vibrant.

They walked into the confectionery shop that was long and narrow. Shelves ran on both sides of the shop and reached up to the tall ceiling. Lining the shelves were matching glass and ceramic jars and containers. The glass jars were filled with a colorful assortment of rock candy, hard candy, jelly candy, candied fruit, glazed fruit, and a large variety of sweets and treats. Under the glass counter were chocolates, fudge, and toffee.

They left the store after purchasing a small bag of caramel and jellybeans.

Next to the confectionary sat a small art gallery. The trio stood looking in the window where a framed picture sat on a brass stand. The painting was a portrait of a young woman in the front window. She had long reddish golden hair and she was lovely, but her beauty was marred by a countenance of sadness. Her hands were pressed, palm to palm as if in prayer, and she laid them against her cheek. The woman carried a forlorn look, her blue-grey eyes, heavy-lidded, were cast down.

The two women were enraptured with the portrait and stood on each side of their male companion and studied the details of the painting.

"Why do you think she is so sad?" Carol asked.

"It could only be love," Miss Hope said.

"Love? How do you mean?" Carol said, looking at Penelope.

"Only love can make a woman feel that way. It must be a lost love—an abandoned love. Her heart is broken, and she cannot even bring herself to consider if it will ever be mended. Her life, her entire being was dependent on that love, and now it is gone. That is why she looks sad. Thus, it is with some women."

Carol turned back to the painting. She saw it now, she felt it. Nodding slowly in agreement, she touched her eye with a gloved hand. A small wet mark appeared there. Carol felt the woman's pain, it was her pain, her abandonment. It was her heart that was broken.

They turned away and walked silently down the street. Soon that heaviness regarding lost love and sadness faded. Conversation resumed. As they walked along, Carol could not help but feel an attachment to everything she saw. It was all connected and she felt that connectedness. It felt glorious. To be part of all there is. Belonging. That is what she felt.

She felt like she belonged here.

They soon found their way back to the bandstand and stepped up into it. In the shade of the bandstand, the two women closed their parasols.

"It is truly a lovely day," Miss Hope said. "It is a shame you must be getting back."

"Yes, it is," Carol said, for she felt as if she could stay here forever. She thought a moment. "Why must I be getting back?"

The couple looked at one another knowingly and smiled.

"Why, Caroline, this was only to be a short visit," Mr. Crawford said. "All visits come to an end."

"But what if I do not wish to go?" Carol said. "Can I not simply stay?"

"You have to go, Caroline," Crawford said.

"You will come back to us soon, I am sure," Miss Hope said, eagerly. "And when you come back, we will introduce you to Mr. Pennington."

"Mr. Pennington?"

"Mr. Walter Pennington," Crawford said. "A truly splendid chap. You will like him."

Miss Hope touched her arm. "Oh, yes, Caroline, you will simply adore him. I know it."

"Must I go now?" Carol asked, with sadness and a hint of desperation.

"We will see each other again, soon. I promise you," Penelope Hope said. She gave Carol a light embrace, touching her cheek with hers.

Robert Crawford tipped his hat to Carol and took Penelope's arm in his.

Carol watched them walk down the street. They did not turn back to look at her. Carol fought off a wave of sadness that threatened to engulf her. She looked around the bandstand which was empty save for herself. She looked up at the roof which consisted of cedar shingles set in a staggering pattern leading to the center. The ceiling appeared to move. It spun slowly and she watched it spin, and as it spun, it appeared to change color and shape. It reminded Carol of a kaleidoscope she had as a child. The ceiling spun faster and faster until she grew quite dizzy.

5

Carol woke up. She was reclined and as she opened her eyes, she took a moment to orient herself. She stared up at the ceiling, the walls. She saw furniture, a picture hung on the wall. Carol knew all these items. She was familiar with them. They were hers. She was in her living room lying on the couch. Somehow everything felt a bit unreal. The early morning sun was coming through the window. Rising slowly to a sitting position, she attempted to make certain she was no longer dreaming. The scene felt unnatural, almost foreign. She touched her face and patted her chest just to feel something. Clearing her throat audibly she said, "Hello," simply to hear her voice. It sounded normal. She touched her face and different parts of her body. It felt right. Across the room, sitting on a chair was her cross-stitch. Carol regarded it with suspicion.

When Carol stood up, her head felt dizzy. She took three panicky deep breaths and waited for the dizziness to pass. Do something normal, she told herself. Go into the kitchen and make some coffee. She obeyed her thoughts.

Almost mechanically and without thinking, she turned on the coffee maker, poured water into the reservoir, took out a coffee pod, inserted it, and pushed the button. Coffee began to spill out, making a mess before she realized she had failed to put a cup under the spout.

"Shit!" she spat. Her mind was not quite right. Her thinking was altered. Her mind was back there, she thought—in Smith Falls. But how could that be? It was only a dream, she reasoned. Only a dream. But it was so real, so vibrant. Carol could remember every detail.

Nausea overcame her. It felt like she had jet lag. She had never experienced jet lag, but she was sure this was what it felt like. Sitting on a kitchen chair Carol put her head between her knees and waited for the feeling to subside.

She continued to feel woozy all that day and part of the next. During that time, she did not work on her cross-stitch, rather, she tried to make sense of her bizarre experience. It was just a dream, she told herself over and over. That explanation did not hold water, however. It was her experience that details of dreams often fade with time if one can remember them at all. How many times had she woken up in the middle of the night from a dream and could remember little or nothing about it by morning? However, her Smith Falls experience was so vivid that she recalled every detail no matter how small, for days. She remembered every smell, every scene, every sensation.

The cross-stitch was never far from her mind, though. Carol knew that she would get back to it. Every day she felt the project pull at her until finally she picked up her needle and resumed her stitching.

There were just over twenty different types of stitches in cross-stitch, and this project called for eight of them. Some of them, such as the French knot, she had never done before, but she found that she mastered it quickly.

Carol was becoming a better cross-stitcher, she knew it—she could see it. Her fingers were nimbler, her eyes more discernible and her stamina was increasing. She found she could cross-stitch for hours and not get tired. It was most addictive. More and more she realized she was creating something very special not normally seen at competitions, particularly at small craft fairs like the one in Bedford. Carol was certain she was creating a blue-ribbon winner.

Her phone rang while she was in mid-stitch. She let out a groan of frustration and put down her work.

"Hello."

"Hello, Carol, it's Amanda. How are you?"

"I'm well, Amanda. How are you?"

"I'm struggling but persevering. You know me. Thanks for asking."

Carol could not help but roll her eyes.

"I'm calling to remind you of the upcoming meeting."

"Is this going to be an ongoing thing now, Amanda?"

"What do you mean?"

"You gave me a reminder call last meeting, and I'll bet you aren't calling any of the others to remind them."

"You have forgotten about meetings in the past, you know."

"One meeting!"

"You know, a poor memory may be indicative of another problem, Carol."

"What?"

"A poor memory might be the side effect of medication. Are you taking any prescribed medication?"

"No."

"It could be brought on by an infection. Do you have an infection?"

"No."

"It could be depression. Are you depressed?"

"Amanda!"

"It's Gary, isn't it?"

"Amanda!"

"Yes, Carol?"

"How are things with Tim?" Carol asked calmly.

"Fine. Why do you ask?"

"Because the last time we got together, you said you thought he was having an affair."

The line went quiet.

"Um… well… I'm still working that out. Yeah…. So, we'll see you at Tina's tomorrow. Did you know it was tomorrow?"

"Yes, Amanda. I am looking at my calendar right now and I have a big X on tomorrow's date," Carol lied.

"It's not tomorrow. It's the day after tomorrow."

"Then why did you say tomorrow?"

"I wanted to know if you truly knew."

"Goodbye, Amanda."

"One o'clock, don't be late."

Carol hung up the phone and decided to get back to her cross-stitch. Two days before the next meeting. She could get a lot done in two days. She was eager to show off her new work to her group.

Carol pulled up in front of Tina's home. It was beautiful. Tina and her husband Vincent DeLuca were active members of the Italian community in Bedford. When they decided to build a house, they were given a lot of support. They got a good deal on a lot in a new suburb of expensive homes. Their Italian contractor gave them a good deal on their new home. It had four bedrooms and four baths and a lot of expensive tile work. Carol thought it was silly having such a big house only for the two of them. Tina and Vincent had no children, and it did not look like they would ever have any. Almost every time Tina spoke of her house, the term 'resale value' always found its way into the conversation. It wasn't a home; it was an investment. It wasn't simply a place where you lived, it was a showpiece—something else to brag about.

Carol and the other ladies parked on the street. Vincent did not want any cars dripping oil on his stone double driveway. When Carol pulled up to the house, she checked her watch. It read 1:05. Getting better, she thought. She got her soft case that contained her framed cross-stitch and enough floss she would need for the afternoon. Carol attempted to hold her excitement in check. She was eager to show her friends her new project and hear what they thought of it. They would love it, of course. Who wouldn't?

She walked up the six stone steps to the covered porch. She rang the bell and stepped in. Everyone was there, of course. Carol was the last to arrive—again. Despite her tardiness, Carol was met by the usual smiles. Tina stepped forward and air-kissed her. Tina was even more made up when she hosted.

"Do be a dear and take off your shoes, please," Tina said. "The floors, you understand."

"I wish I had brought slippers," Carol said, slipping off her shoes.

"I have these for you," Tina said, with a smile, and held up a pair of pink knitted slippers. "I made them myself. I made a pair for all of us."

Only now did Carol see the other three women were all wearing the same knitted slippers. Only Tina wore shoes—a very handsome two-tone pair of pumps, which matched her dress perfectly.

As Carol approached, Amanda announced with a big smile, "I feel the itch—the itch to stitch!"

Carol did not seem to mind Amanda's goofy catchphrase today. Today, nothing was going to bother her.

They all went into the living room and began to unpack their crafts. Tina was standing by her side before Carol had her cross-stitch out of its case.

"I wanted to show you this cross-stitch I told you about," Tina said, holding a framed cross-stitch.

Carol saw that this was the same cross-stitch of flowers in a vase that she was working on at their last meeting. It looked very good.

"You see, I told you I did this years ago," Tina said.

"Yes, I remember. You told me."

"But I wanted you to see it. Get yours out and we can compare them."

Carol knew exactly why Tina wanted to compare them—so she could show how much better hers was.

"I don't have it with me," Carol said. "I gave up on that and started something new."

"Oh," Tina said, sad she could not show up Carol's work. "What are you working on now?"

Carol slid her cross-stitch out of her carrying case. She stood up and held it for Tina to see.

"You did this?" Tina said. She sounded almost shocked. "I cannot believe you did this."

The way Tina said it was like getting a compliment and an insult at the same time. Tina reached to take the frame.

Carol tightened her grip on it. "I'll hold it."

By now the other women came over to have a look. Their eyes opened wide in amazement. Compliments came flooding out. Carol took it all in and reveled in the attention and praise until she was almost dizzy. There were endless questions about the cross-stitch. Where did you find it? What type of stitches are you using? What kind of floss is that? Is that Jobelan? What is the count?"

"It's a forty-count."

"There is no such thing as a forty-count," Tina said, haughtily.

"No?" was all Carol said.

"It's hard to believe you got this much done since our last meeting," said Margaret. She cocked her head and regarded the work. "Huh," she said enigmatically as if she was not certain what to make of it. Margaret turned away with an almost troubled expression.

"Yes, it is hard to believe you were able to do this since last we met," Tina said with a hint of doubt.

Did Tina think Carol was trying to take credit for someone else's work, Carol thought.

"I think it is quite lovely," Harriet said. "Where did you say you got it?"

Carol froze. She was reluctant to reveal where she got the cross-stitch. Generally, information like that was readily shared in craft groups. One of the things about these groups was not just the camaraderie—women coming together in friendship—but also sharing cross-stitching tips and information. But in this case, Carol did not wish any of the women, especially Tina, to know about Malum Crafts. It was to remain her little secret. What if they were to go there and get one like it? Then Carol's work would not be special at all. Her work would not stand out or be the envy of the group.

No—this was Carol's moment to shine, and she had no intention of giving up or sharing any of the limelight. She simply did not respond to Harriet's question and made out as if she had not heard it.

Never had Carol enjoyed a cross-stitch meeting more than this one. She was open with comments and listened to the other women. Most of them asked Carol her opinion regarding the cross-stitch they were working on. She gave it freely, feeling she was now a much better stitcher than a month ago. To Carol, everyone seemed more open and happier—everyone except Tina. She could see Tina was uncomfortable. Carol often caught Tina looking over at her and her cross-stitch, and in that look was both suspicion and envy. That suited Carol just fine.

"Where did you say you found that?" Tina asked. "Was it Michales… Hobby Lobby?"

"No, it wasn't one of those," Carol said, looking as if she was struggling to remember.

"Then, where was it?" Tina asked, not willing to let it go.

"Um… it was a small place. I can't remember the name of it."

"Where is it?"

"It is north of Manchester," Carol said, giving the opposite direction.

"North of Manchester? What were you doing up there?"

"You know, it was a month ago, and I wasn't even looking for a craft store. I think I got lost on a back road and came across it quite by accident and decided to go in and look around.

"And you can't think of the name of this store?" Tina asked.

Carol stopped her stitching and looked as if she was trying her best to remember. "I seem to recall the name started with a C or a G. I can't remember exactly."

"Well, I think it is glorious," Harriet said. "You're not even done, but I just know that if you enter that in the craft show—any craft show—it's sure to win first prize!

"You really think so?" Carol said as if she hadn't even thought about it.

"Oh, dear, yes."

"It's sure to win 2nd place, anyway," Amanda said.

Carol turned to Amanda. The woman could not help but say the wrong thing.

After some time, Tina announced she was going to put out some refreshments. Carol felt generous and asked Tina if she needed any help. Tina turned down her help and said she could handle it herself.

As one might expect, Tina's refreshments surpassed everyone's. There was a shrimp ring, a delicious cheese ball Tina made herself, and an avocado dip. Carol complimented Tina on everything, especially the sangria made from a recipe, Tina said, that she picked up when she and Vincent were in Spain.

"Would it be all right if I borrow that pattern when you're done?" Tina asked Carol.

Carol almost froze. She remembered the instructions prohibited her from giving away parts of the craft to anyone. To be totally honest, she should not have even shown the cross-stitch to anyone, not even her friends.

"Uhm...," was all she could say.

"I know they have big copiers that would take that size. Why don't we just copy it?"

"I'll tell you what, Tina. I'll have it copied and give you one. If anyone else wants a copy, let me know." Carol said this as sincerely as she could but knew she had no intention of making a copy for anyone.

After the refreshments, talk turned away from Carol and her cross-stitch, so she attempted to steer it back in that direction.

"You know, I have become so absorbed in this work, that I dreamed about it the other day." As soon as she got the words out, she regretted it.

The other women looked at her.

"That's something," said Margaret in her taciturn manner.

"What was the dream about?" Harriet asked.

Carol shrugged and groped for a response. "I truly can't recall. You know how dreams are—they fade quickly. All I remember is it was about the cross-stitch."

In truth, Carol remembered every detail of the dream as if it had truly happened. She would have loved to tell these women—she would have loved to tell anyone—of her visit to Smith Falls and meeting and talking to the young couple. For some reason, she felt she could not tell her friends the details of the dream—if indeed it was a dream. Of course, it was a dream—what else could it have been?

When it came time, the women began to pack up and everyone thanked Tina for such a lovely time. Margaret and Harriet were the first to depart, as they arrived together in the same car. They left their knitted slippers at the door.

"Carol, could you stay and give me a hand to clean up a bit?" Tina asked.

"I could stay," Amanda chimed.

"Honey, that's sweet, but Carol and I can handle things," Tina said. "It's not so much for the two of us. You run along and thanks. It was wonderful seeing you."

Amanda seemed crestfallen as she changed from her slippers to her shoes and said goodbye.

"Carol, would you be a dear and rinse those dishes and put them in the dishwasher? Thanks so much."

Tina went back into the living room while Carol cleared the dishes from the Cambria countertop and rinsed them in the deep under-mount porcelain sink. The kitchen window looked out over the backyard. It could be considered acreage being as big as it was. Most of these lots were quite substantial.

Carol had stacked all the dishes by the time Tina returned with a few other dishes and the leftover carrot cake she had served after the other refreshments.

"Great! Thanks, Carol. It was a fun get-together, wasn't it?" Tina said.

"Yes, you were the consummate hostess."

"That is kind of you to say." Tina appeared to hesitate.
"Was there something else?"
Tina thought as if she were struggling with what she wanted to say.
"What did you think about what Amanda said at the last meeting?"
Carol shook her head to say she did not remember.
"What she said about her husband having an affair—do you think there is anything in it?"
Carol clenched her teeth which looked like a cross between a grimace and a smile. "You know Amanda. She's a bit of a crisis junkie. Sometimes she sees things that aren't there. I'm not saying she was making it up, I'm just saying she might be exaggerating the facts."
"You truly think so?"
Carol nodded.
"That is a bit of a relief. I'm so glad we spoke."
Carol was a bit surprised that Tina had wanted to speak to her in confidence. She seldom saw this side of her."
"There wasn't anything like that between you and Gary, was there?" Tina asked.
"What?" This caught Carol by surprise.
"Gary wasn't seeing anyone while you two were married, was he? I mean, I know he is seeing someone now, but—"
"No, Tina. He wasn't seeing anyone while we were married." Now this was the Tina she knew.
"I am so relieved to hear you say that," Tina said. "I do care about you. I care about all of you. Sometimes I think that if Vincent ever cheated on me, I would kill him."
Carol believed her. "Let's hope it doesn't come to that," she said trying to smile.
Tina asked, "Where did we say next time?"
"Harriet's."
"Yes, of course. Well, that's great. I'll see you out."
Carol grabbed her craft case. On her way to the door, she slid on the tile floor and almost fell. She gasped and reached for the wall to steady herself.

"Are you all right, sweetie?" Tina said coming to her side and lending an arm.

"Yes," Carol said, righting herself and catching her breath. "That tile is slippery."

"It's those slippers. Harriet slipped and almost fell earlier. I am going to put rubber grippers on the bottom for the next time you all come. I don't want anyone to fall on this floor. That is the thing about tile; it can be slippery, and if someone were to fall, they could hurt themselves, and I would hate to be sued."

"Well, I'm fine. I won't sue you."

"I am so glad."

At the door, Carol changed out of her slippers and into her shoes. After a hug and a goodbye, Carol was out the door and headed to her car. Once in the vehicle she put her craft bag on the seat next to her and started the engine. She was about to put the car in gear but hesitated. She was not certain why she did. She looked at her craft bag. Carol was certain she had zipped it closed, but now it was partly opened. A feeling of uneasiness came over her. She could not explain it. Carol unzipped the bag and hurriedly looked through it. Her pattern was missing. How could that be? She distinctly remembered putting the pattern in the case. She had put everything in the case. A slight wave of panic passed over her. Tina! Tina took the pattern*! Please, stay and help me clean up. I wanted to ask you about Amanda.* What a sneaky, manipulative, little—.

Carol shut off the engine and jumped out of the car and ran up the driveway to the front door. She almost knocked. No, Tina doesn't deserve any courtesy. She bounded through the door. Tina stepped out of the living room to see who had come in. She was holding the pattern in her hands. Seeing it was Carol, she quickly hid the paper behind her.

"Give it back!" Carol shouted. "You had no right to take it! Give it back, it's mine!"

Carol rushed at Tina who had taken a few steps back on the tile floor.

Tina, without knowing it, could ruin everything for her, Carol thought. Or maybe she knew it. Maybe Tina was so jealous that she knew exactly what she was doing.

"I only wished to copy it!" Tina said. "You said I could have a copy!"

The two women struggled over the pattern. Tina was strong, but Carol fought in a frenzy. Carol grabbed Tina's hands and using her hip she turned Tina suddenly. Tina lost her footing and her head slammed into the edge of two walls. She fell and hit her head on the tile floor. The sound of her head striking the tile was sickening.

Carol straightened and looked down at her. Tina was not moving. A trickle of blood ran onto the floor. Carol continued to stare down at her in shock. She looked at the pattern in her hand. There was no sound in the house but her own breathing. Carol started to shake. Fear gripped her and she was afraid she would be blamed for this—feared she would have to reveal why the pattern was so important to her. She could not be a part of this. Run. She had to run. With the pattern in hand, she made for the door. Looking down she saw the four pairs of knitted slippers. Acting quickly, but not thinking clearly, she grabbed a pair of slippers, went back to where Tina lay, then slipped off Tina's shoes and placed the slippers on her feet. On her way out of the house, Carol dropped Tina's shoes by the door.

Carol opened the door slowly and looked out. As before the street appeared empty, but she could not be certain. She took two deep breaths and stepped out, closed the door, and then turned back and said, "Goodbye." as naturally as she could. With her heart racing and her entire body shaking, as calmly as she could, Carol walked to her car, got in, started the engine, and drove away.

6

Carol's hands trembled all during the drive home. Her mind swirled and spun. Once while stopped by a red light, she was not aware that it changed to green. A driver behind her leaned on his horn long enough to prompt her to go. Once, she came close to hitting another car. She should not have been driving. Carol pulled over into a parking lot and stopped. She had put the pattern on the passenger seat. With trembling hands, she put the pattern into her craft case. Carol realized she was not yet ready to drive, so she decided to get out of the car. Without knowing it, she had pulled into a small shopping mall. Grabbing her purse and craft case, Carol decided to go into the mall and walk off her distress. She hoped she wouldn't throw up.

In the mall, Carol walked and looked in the windows of stores. She was not aware of what she was looking at. She moved about puppet-like, practically mindless. Nothing registered. Before long, she stood in front of a small craft store. She went inside.

"Can I help you with anything?"

A woman came out from behind the counter and addressed Carol. Carol regarded the woman as if she did not understand what she'd said.

"Can I help you with anything?" the woman repeated.

"No. Thank you. I'm just looking."

Carol went up and down the aisles. She looked at her watch. For some reason, she thought it would be good to establish an alibi. Picking up some cross-stitch needles and some floss she went to the counter to pay for it.

"Didn't you used to work at Michaels?" she said to the woman behind the counter.

The woman looked at her and smiled. "No. I've never worked there."

"The Michaels in Amherst, not the one in Manchester," Carol said.

"I've never worked at any of the Michaels stores," the woman insisted.

"Funny, I could have sworn it was you. Do you have the time?"

"It's just about 4:30."

"Thank you."

Carol would be sure to hang on to the receipt. She might need it. There was also a very good chance the cashier would remember her coming into the store and acting quite naturally, and not like a person who had just witnessed someone receiving serious head trauma.

Carol soon left the store and stopped by a coffee shop and ordered a coffee. She would have preferred to have a stiff drink. As soon as she got home that is exactly what she would do.

Carol drank half her coffee before she decided she was well enough to drive home. She got in her car and held her hands out in front of her, fingers spread. They still trembled, but not as bad as before. Taking some deep breaths, she started to drive. When she came home, her neighbor, Susan, was out front of her house. Carol parked in the driveway and walked over to Susan to make small talk. She needed to appear calm and that nothing of terrible consequence had occurred. Later she barely remembered the conversation.

Once inside her house, Carol poured herself that drink. She drank it down and poured another. She sat in her kitchen and did not know what to do. She could not justify her actions at Tina's. She felt torn. Sleep was out of the question. Her mind was spinning so much. After her third drink, she stopped.

She decided to call Amanda and have a chitchat as if everything was normal.

Amanda did not answer. Carol called Harriet. No answer. What are the odds that neither of them picked up? Carol did not want to call Margaret; it would be uncharacteristic. She rarely called Margaret. A flash of brilliance. She would call Tina. If ever her phone records were checked, they would show that when she came home, Carol phoned her friends. How natural. She even called Tina like there was nothing wrong at all. No one would think that Carol would call Tina after leaving her unconscious and bleeding on the floor. Her stomach turned. She called Tina and let it ring for a time. Then she thought, what if someone answers? She hung up the phone.

Do phone calls register if the call doesn't go through? She didn't know.

She decided to try Amanda again. Amanda answered.

"Hello, Amanda, it's Carol—" She froze. She did not plan on what she was going to say.

"Are you there, Carol?"

"Yes, I'm here. I…" Try to sound calm and natural, she thought. "Did you just get home?"

"A short while ago. Are you all right, Carol?"

"Oh, yes, I'm fine. What a good group today."

"Yes, it was."

"Listen, Amanda, I hope I didn't sound too testy to you about those reminders that you give me. I mean… I hope I didn't hurt your feelings or anything."

"Oh, that's all right. Don't worry about it."

"That's all I wanted to say. It was on my heart and mind, and I just wanted to say if I came off… you know… angry or testy… I didn't mean it. Okay?"

"Okay."

"Okay. Well, I… I'll call you again soon. Goodbye."

"Goodbye, Carol."

I hope that sounded normal, she thought.

Carol paced about the house like some kind of caged animal. She was so uncertain of what to do. Best do nothing. Nothing. She turned on the television and eventually fell asleep.

Carol woke up early. She showered and got ready for work. She was waiting in the parking lot in front of Crafty Business when Irene Weston arrived to open.

"I'm surprised to see you here this early," Irene said.

"Just trying to make up for my past sins," Carol said and instantly regretted it.

"Past sins? What do you mean?"

"You know, all the times I was late, or left early."

Irene thought this a bit out of character for Carol and was somewhat confused by her behavior.

"What do you need to be done first," Carol said, once they were inside.

All that day, Irene suspected something was bothering Carol. She worked, almost nonstop, going from one job to the other. When a customer entered the store, Carol was right there to help them.

In the afternoon, Irene mentioned to Caril that she could leave for the day if she wished. Carol told her that she would stay until close, and then she went to restock some shelves.

Irene knew Carol fairly well. Their relationship went back about six years. She had never seen Carol like this, but her behavior was easy to read. *Trying to make up for my past sins*, she had said. Carol was attempting to work off some penance. She had done something wrong and was hoping to atone. Irene found it hard to believe this was all about Carol's absenteeism and tardiness.

"Perhaps I owe you an apology, Carol," Irene said to her before they prepared to close. "When we spoke before about your cross-stitch skills, I may have been too harsh. I apologize for those remarks."

"Thank you, Irene. Let's not talk anymore about it—water under the bridge."

When she arrived home, Carol was still sorely distressed. How could she have left Tina like that? She must have been out of her mind—insane! Under any other circumstances, Carol would have never acted in such a despicable manner. It was the cross-stitch—that is what caused her to act that way.

Carol found her craft case where she left it and put it and its contents in the back of her bedroom closet.

The next day Carol got a call from Amanda.

"Carol, have you heard?" Amanda said, her voice trembling. "It's terrible, it's just terrible! Poor Tina! I can't believe it."

"Calm down, Amanda, and explain to me what you are talking about."

"It's about Tina. They think she fell in the hallway of her house and struck her head. She's in the hospital. The doctors said she received a concussion and she's in a coma."

"A coma? Do they think she'll come out of the coma?"

"They don't know. It's very bad."

"A police detective has been here. He's already talked to Harriet and Margaret."

"A police detective? What did he want?"

"He asked questions about our last meeting. That was the day Tina was found. Vincent came home from work and found her unconscious and bleeding on the tile floor. Whatever happened, must have happened soon after we left."

"What do you think happened?"

"I don't know. But I must go now. The detective asked that I don't call you."

"Why not?"

"He's on his way over to talk to you. Bye."

Carol's heart raced as she fought against the urge to panic. She took some Benadryl and tidied up the place.

The doorbell rang, and she answered it. The police detective was an average-looking man about forty years of age. There was nothing very distinctive about him—not too tall, not too thin, he had brown hair and brown eyes, and was dressed well enough in a brown suit and tie. He certainly liked brown. His most distinguishing characteristic was that he gave the impression that he did not wish to be here. Almost like it was a waste of his time.

"Are you Carol Crane?" he asked. His tone was apathetic.

"Yes."

"I'm Detective Mike Jarmon, from the Manchester Police Department," he said holding up his identification.

"Yes?"

"I would like to ask you some questions about Tina DeLuca. Have you heard what happened to her?"

"No," she lied.

"May I come in?"

"Yes, of course."

Carol ushered Det. Jarmon into the living room. He gave the surroundings a cursory assessment. They're trained to do that, Carol mused.

"Would you care to sit down?" she asked.

"Thank you."

"Would you like something to drink? A glass of water or a soft drink, perhaps?"

"Do you have coffee on?"

"Yes. Well, I mean I can make you a coffee."

"Don't go to any trouble."

"No trouble. I use those coffee pods. It takes a minute. Excuse me." Carol went into the kitchen to make coffee, and Jarmon followed her.

"Nice place," he said. "Do you live here alone?"

She cast him a questioning glance.

"You're not wearing a wedding ring," he said. "But there is still something of a tan line."

"I used to be married. I'm recently divorced."

"Sorry."

"Me too. So, what's this all about? Did something happen to Tina?"

He did not answer her question but took out a notebook and pen. He made notes during the interview with Carol.

"You and Tina DeLuca and some other women belong to a craft club?" He said it more as an assertion than a question.

"Yes. We meet about once a month. We get together to cross-stitch."

"When was the last time you got together?"

"Two days ago. But I think you already know that."

He looked at her with a bit of a smile. "How would I know about that, Ms. Crane?"

"All right, I'll be honest. Amanda Simon phoned me just before you arrived."

"I asked her not to do that."

"Well, that's Amanda. She likes to be first with the latest news—good or bad."

"What did she tell you?"

"That Tina fell and hit her head and that she is in the hospital in a coma."

"I am afraid so. She was found by her husband when he came home from work. Luckily, he came home and found her when he did. Any later and she might have died."

"Oh, dear. Poor Tina." This made Carol feel even guiltier.

"What time did you and the other ladies arrive at the meeting that day?"

"About one o'clock in the afternoon," she said, handing him his coffee. "Would you like anything for your coffee? Cream or sugar?"

"No, black is fine." He took a sip. "Hot!"

"Yes, sorry. This machine runs very hot."

"I should get one of those," he said, looking at the appliance. Turning back to Carol, he said, "One o'clock. Is that the usual time you have your meetings?"

"Yes. We've been getting together for a couple of years now."

"Do you always meet at the DeLuca residence for your craft club?"

"No, we rotate from house to house."

"Whose turn was it last month?"

"Amanda's"

"That would be Amanda Simons."

"Yes, that's right."

"Whose turn is it next month?"

"Harriet Turner's. Is all this important?

"Probably not. You arrived at the Deluca residence at 1:00. What time did you leave?"

"About 4:00. It is usually from one till four."

"Did you all leave together?"

Carol looked just over his head and thought. "Harriet and Margaret left first at four. Amanda a few minutes later. I left, maybe ten minutes after that."

"So, you were the last one to see Mrs. DeLuca."

"I suppose I was."

"Any reason why you stayed longer?"

"Tina asked me to—to help clean up a bit."

"You helped clean up and then you left?"

"Yes. It was sometime after 4:00."

"Was it 4:10 or 4:30…."

"4:10."

"How did Mrs. DeLuca seem when you left? Was she upset in any way? Did she appear preoccupied?"

"No. She appeared fine. Could you tell me what happened?"

"As I said, Mr. DeLuca came home from work soon after 6:00, about two hours after you left, and he found his wife unconscious on the floor."

"What do you think happened?"

"There was a mark on the edge of the wall near where she had fallen. We figure she somehow hit her head on the edge, fell, and hit her head hard on the tile floor. Cracked it open."

"That is just terrible. So, it was an accident then?"

"It could be."

"I am surprised that the Manchester police are investigating an accident."

"We investigate accidents; besides, I said it could be an accident."

"What else could it be?"

Jarmon looked at Carol with a deadpan expression. From his behavior, Carol thought Jarmon knew exactly what had occurred. But how could he?

"We found some knitted slippers by the door in the DeLuca home," he continued, ignoring her question. "Did you see them when you were there?"

Carol suspected Jarmon knew all about the slippers. He most likely had asked the others the same questions.

"Yes. Tina knitted them herself for all of us. She didn't like guests wearing shoes in the house, and she did not want our feet to get cold. Very thoughtful, actually. When we left Tina's, we left the slippers by the door."

"Did Mrs. DeLuca wear a pair of slippers at your get-together?"

"No. She wore a very nice pair of two-tone shoes."

"That's strange because when Mrs. DeLuca was found, she was wearing a pair of slippers on her feet."

"That is not so strange," Carol said. "After we left, she likely wanted to take off those shoes and put on something comfortable."

"Here is the strange part," Jarmon said. "Four of you ladies wore the slippers, correct? Well, we only found three pairs of slippers at the door. That means Mrs. DeLuca went to the front door, kicked off her shoes where you all deposited your slippers, and picked up a pair and put them on."

Carol furrowed her brow and asked, "What is so strange about that?"

"I don't know. It sounds strange to me—putting on a pair of slippers that someone else wore. But then again, I don't know much about women."

"You're married, aren't you?"

"No, I'm not."

"You were married?"

"No, I have been a bachelor all my life."

"But you're wearing a wedding band on your left-hand ring finger."

Jarmon held up his left hand. "This was my father's wedding band. He did not have much, but he left me this. I wear it in his memory. My ring finger is the only finger it fits."

"You could have it sized to fit any finger you like."

"Yes, I could."

His coffee now sufficiently cooled; Jarmon took a drink. "Good coffee."

"Thanks."

"So, it appears, Mrs. DeLuca put on a pair of slippers, and true to their name she slipped on the tile, hit her head on the corner of the wall, then fell and cracked her head on the tile floor."

"I just can't believe it."

"When I spoke with Harriet Wolters, she said that while at the DeLuca home, she slipped on the tile floor and almost fell while wearing a pair of slippers."

"Oh, my. I only now recall that the same thing happened to me."

"You too?"

"Yes, I remember, it was right in front of Tina, and she said that the next time we came she would have rubber grips on the bottom so that doesn't happen again."

"She said that?"

"Yes. It is so tragic."

"Now there is another strange thing."

"What's that?"

"Well, Mrs. DeLuca was aware the slippers were slippery on the tile floor, yet she put on a pair and fell."

"As I said, it is so, so tragic."

"It is surely one for the books," he said, shaking his head.

They sat looking at one another, and Carol was certain Jarmon suspected her. Yet, how could he?

"So, you left the DeLuca home at 4:10," Jarmon said, looking over his notes. "Where did you go after that?"

"After that? I came home. No, wait. I stopped by Southland Mall."

"Why did you do that?"

"Why? Because I had spent the entire afternoon sitting and I wanted to walk about a bit."

"Did you go in any store?"

Carol nodded slowly. "A small craft store. I looked around."

"Did you buy anything?"

"Yes. I bought a few items and left."

"Did you go anywhere else?"

"I stopped for a coffee in the mall."

He made a note of it.

"Do you really need to know all that?" she asked.

"I thank you for your time, Ms. Crane. I'm sorry to bother you with this. I'm sure it is exactly what it looks like—an accident. Just between you and me, Mr. DeLuca is friendly with the police chief in Manchester, and he asked that his wife's fall be investigated. I have to have all this information for my report to prove I sufficiently investigated it. You know what I mean. I am sorry for what happened to your friend."

"Thank you, Det. Jarmon."

He looked inside his empty coffee cup.

"Would you like another?" she asked.

"No, I'd better not. I would like to show you something," he said, and reaching into his pocket, Jarmon took out a small, clear plastic sealed bag. It was like a small Ziplock bag.

"Do you know what this is?"

He handed the small bag to Carol and told her not to take it out. Inside the bag, she could see the torn corner of a piece of paper.

"It looks like the torn corner of a chart," she said.

"Chart?"

"Yes, the paper pattern used to cross-stitch. Do you see these squares? They are part of a grid pattern like the cloth used in cross-stitch."

"That is what the other ladies in your craft club told me," he said. "This piece of paper was found clutched in Mrs. DeLuca's hand."

Carol felt her heart sink. She remembered her struggle with Tina over her pattern. She felt hot. Carol fought for control and hoped she was not displaying any sign of anxiety.

"Could you show me the chart of the cross-stitch you were working on that day," Jarmon asked in a friendly manner.

"Of course," she said and went to her bedroom. She returned holding a craft bag and put it on the kitchen table. Carol unzipped the bag, removed her cross-stitch project, and then the pattern. She handed it to Jarmon.

He unfolded the chart and scrutinized it. "This is your current project?" he asked and read the title on the chart. "Flowers in a Vase". He examined the four corners of the chart. It was intact—no rips or tears. He picked up the cross-stitch. "Very nice. I like it."

"Perhaps when I am finished, I will make you a gift of it."

"That is very kind, but not necessary. Again, thank you for your time, and I hope your friend fully recovers. When she does, she can tell us exactly what happened."

7

Carol stood by the closed door, shaking. It was everything she could do to escort Jarmon to the door and see him out. As he got in his car, she gave him a final wave and closed the door. Now she found she could not move. She rested her head against the door. She tried to think. What should she do? What could she do? A sharp rap on the door startled her. The knock felt like it went right into her forehead. Who is it now? she thought. Can't I just have a little peace?

With a few deep breaths, Carol opened the door and was surprised to see Det. Jarmon standing there. He looked at Carol with suspicion.

"Sorry to bother you again, Ms. Crane," he said. "I thought you might want to know about Mrs. DeLuca. She's at the Catholic Medical Center in Manchester on McGregor Street. I'm sure you meant to ask."

"Yes. Yes, of course, I did. I was just so aghast at what happened to poor Tina."

He nodded. "I'm sure that was it."

"Thank you, Det. Jarmon. I appreciate your concern."

Jarmon left a second time. Carol went to the kitchen, took another Benadryl, and washed it down with gin.

That was a foolish thing to do, she thought. She didn't care. She felt she needed it. She couldn't crumble now. Now she had to do something a normal person who did not feel guilty would do. What would a normal person who did not feel guilty do in such circumstances? They would call their friend to commiserate.

With her phone in her hand, Carol sat on her sofa. Who should she call first?

The phone rang in her hand, which startled her yet again. Carol felt like a bundle of exposed nerves. She let it ring twice before she answered.

"Hello, Carol, it's Amanda."

Of course.

"Hello, Amanda."

"Did the— "

"He just left."

"What did he say to you?"

"The same thing he said to you, I suppose."

"Isn't it just awful about Tina? How could this have happened?"

"The police figure Tina put on a pair of those slippers after we left, she slipped on the tile floor, hit her head, then fell and hit her head again on the floor."

"I can hardly believe it."

"Neither can I."

"What did you think of that detective, Jarmon?"

"What about him?"

"He gave me the creeps. The way he talked he sounded as if one of us had something to do with Tina getting hurt."

"He said that?"

"No. It was the way he talked. His questions sounded… accusatorial."

"I didn't notice."

"The four of us should send flowers to Tina's room. They may not be allowing any visitors."

"Yes, sending flowers is a good idea. Perhaps one of us should call Vincent. He doesn't need to hear from all four of us at a time like this."

"I'll call Vincent if you want."

"That's good of you, Amanda."

"Should I call today or wait a day or two?"

"Maybe you should wait."

"Carol, did Tina say anything to you before you left her house?"

"Such as what?"

"I don't know. Did she say if she was expecting anyone? A visitor or an appointment, perhaps?"

"A visitor or an appointment? Amanda, what are you saying?"

"It was almost two hours from the time we left until the time Vincent came home."

"Two hours—so what? What are you trying to say?"

"Carol, do you think Tina may have been attacked by someone after we all left her house?"

"Oh, gee, Amanda, I don't know. The police don't seem to think so. Did you say any of this to Jarmon?"

"No. The police don't need any help from me. They consider all types of possibilities."

The line went silent.

"What are you going to do now?" Amanda asked.

"I am going to call the other women."

"Who will you call first?"

"What possible difference can that make?"

"If you call Margaret first, I'll call Harriet."

"I plan on calling Harriet as soon as you and I hang up."

"Oh… well… goodbye then,"

Carol called up Harriet right away. Their conversation was similar to the one between Carol and Amanda. Harriet said they should all pray for Tina's full recovery, and that she had already been to church to light a candle for Tina.

"We should all get together soon, the four of us. I think we need each other at a time like this."

"Yes, of course," Carol agreed. "Have you spoken with the others—Margaret and Amanda?"

"Yes, I have. I think we're all very upset over this situation."

"Amanda said something strange to me today. Well, not strange, exactly. She said that Tina may have had contact with someone from the time we left, and the time Vincent came home. Do you think there is anything in that?"

Harriet paused in thought. "Tina was a bit made-up; I'll admit that. Do you mean she was expecting a man—like having an affair?"

"I don't know. It was just something Amanda said, and it made me think."

"Amanda has an imagination. We all know that. Still, how well do you know anyone? Amanda told me that Tina had asked you to stay that day to straighten up. Did she give you the impression she was expecting anyone that afternoon?"

Carol hesitated. Here was her chance to sow seeds of suspicion away from herself. She must be careful, however. She did not mention anything of the like to Det. Jarmon and it might be suspicious if she added it to her statement now. The story could get complicated. Best to keep it as close to the truth as possible. People would have their suspicions without her prompting them.

"She didn't imply she was expecting anyone that afternoon," Carol said. "I know you and Margaret are close, how is she taking it?"

"You know Margaret. She doesn't say much, but she did say she would pray for Tina."

"I was going to call her."

"You should, but I do not believe she is home just now. I tried her phone at the apartment, and she didn't pick up. She doesn't have a cell."

"I'll try to call her later."

"All right, honey. We'll get together soon. Goodbye."

Carol remained sitting on the couch, thinking. The entire matter was horrific and becoming unmanageable for her. So much deception. She was not used to that. She would have to stay on her toes with every conversation with the ladies. And Vincent—how could she ever face Vincent? But what about Tina? She was in a coma, but people come out of comas, don't they? When Tina regains consciousness, she'll tell everyone what truly happened and then Carol will be exposed. How could she explain that she left Tina bleeding on the floor and never called for help? Worse than that, she lied about everything. She put slippers on Tina's feet to cover up her negligence and to throw suspicion off herself. This would be the biggest scandal in Bedford, maybe in all of New Hampshire. It will be on the news, maybe even national news.

Slow down, slow down, slow down. Don't get too far ahead of yourself, she thought. Maybe Tina won't come out of her coma. Don't some people stay in comas for years? Didn't she once hear of a Canadian woman who woke up from a coma after twenty-nine years? Twenty-nine years—Carol would be just over sixty. She could move away, change her name and appearance, and maybe they would never find her. Wait a minute. Maybe she doesn't have to worry about that. A bad head injury like Tina's could bring on amnesia. If she comes out of a coma, she may never remember what happened. True amnesia is rare, but it could happen. What if it is only temporary amnesia? That means Carol would have to spend her life waiting for Tina to remember. It would be like living with a ticking time bomb.

Carol thought of her conversations with Jarmon, Amanda, and Harriet. She replayed them over in her mind of what was said. When she spoke with Amanda and Harriet, Carol did not mention the torn piece of chart Jarmon had shown her. Indeed, he mentioned that he had shown it to at least one of the ladies. Maybe he had asked all of them about it. He had said they told him it was from a chart. That scrap of paper could be her undoing.

Carol went into her closet and took out the craft case. She had a few of them, but this was the biggest one. Setting the case on the bed, she unzipped it and removed the Smith Fall's chart. Unfolding it she saw what she knew she would see. The righthand lower corner of the chart was missing a piece. It had torn off in Tina's hand when they struggled for it. Carol knew the torn piece of chart Jarmon had shown her would fit perfectly. Her heart sank. She did not think it was possible to feel worse, but she did. This was evidence. How could she explain a torn piece of the chart being found in Tina's hand? I had forgotten my chart and Tina was handing it to me and it tore. She must have kept it in her hand until after I left, and she was still holding it when she slipped and fell. A five-year-old child wouldn't believe that lie.

She could throw away the chart. That was one solution. But if she did, she would never be able to finish the cross-stitch, and she desperately needed to finish it. But the longer she kept it, the better the chances of someone seeing it and making that connection. She would finish the cross-stitch in private. It would never leave her home. When the group got together, Carol would work on other projects, such as Flowers in a Vase. No one would see Smith Falls until it was completed and by then she could dispose of the chart.

No, better. She had an idea. Carol would take the chart to a copying center, and get it copied. The copy would be blank where the tear existed on the original. Then, using a pencil— no better, a pen— and a ruler, she could fill in the missing squares and it would look just like the original. She would get it copied two-sided so the rules would be there. That way, if Jarmon asked any of the ladies in the group if this were the chart they saw her use, it would look exactly like it to them. After all, they only saw it at one meeting.

Carol got another craft case, this one smaller. In it, she put in the torn chart along with two other charts so it would appear she was simply copying some of her patterns. That wasn't uncommon. She decided she would find a copying store in Manchester where no one would know her.

The next day, Carol drove to Manchester. Consulting Google, she chose Copy Express on Elm Street in the north part of the city. There was angled parking on the street, and she found an open spot near the store. It was a nice little store on a nice street lined with small trees. The store was empty save for the young copy and print associate behind the counter. He met Carol with a smile.

"Good morning," she said. "I would like some copies made." Reaching into her craft bag she pulled out the Smith Falls chart and handed it to him. "I need a copy of this. It is a little big."

"No problem," he said looking at it. "We have a copier that can handle this size. It'll just be a minute."

He went over, placed the chart under the cover, and selected the size.

"Do you only want one copy?" he asked.

Carol thought. "You know what, let's make it two copies, and I would like them double-sided."

"Two it is and double-sided."

Carol looked out the window, onto the street. She tried to appear calm, but she was nervous like a bad shoplifter getting ready to steal something.

"Umph," the man exclaimed.

Carol turned around and saw he was looking at the two sheets of paper that came out of the machine.

"Let's try that again," he said.

The copy and print associate pushed some buttons and the paper shot out. He shook his head. The young man tried again. He opened the cover and took out the original. The man held it up and examined it. He felt the paper between his fingers and held it up to the light, tilting it this way and that.

"Where did you get this?" he asked.

"Why? Is there a problem?"

"I can't seem to copy it," he said, showing Carol the paper that came out of the machine. They were all blank. "I've never seen this before. I've never even heard of it."

"Is the machine out of ink, or whatever it uses?" Carol asked.

"Well, let's see. Do you have another sheet you would like to copy?"

He handed the Smith Falls chart to Carol and she gave him a chart of Flowers in a Vase that she had brought along.

"How many copies of this one would you like?"

"Two."

He put in the original and pressed some buttons. The machine shot out two sheets. He held them up for Carol to see. They were perfect copies. He handed them to her, and she stared at them open-mouthed.

"Could it be the machine?"

He stifled a smile. "I think we just proved it isn't the machine."

"Could you try a different machine, please?"

She handed him the Smith Falls chart. He accepted it reluctantly and used a different machine. The result was the same—it would not copy.

"Is there anything else I can help you with today?" he said.

"No. No thanks."

He only charged Carol for the two copies of Flowers in a Vase. It did not amount to very much.

With her charts back in her case, Carol walked out. She considered going to another copy place. Stepping onto the sidewalk she stopped short when she heard someone call her name. Turning slowly, she saw Margaret and Harriet walking toward her. No, no, no, no. Not now. Carol could barely move. She felt like she was caught doing something illegal.

"Fancy meeting you here," Harriet said, smiling. Margaret had no smile. "We were driving by when Margaret said, 'That's Carol's car'. Just like that, 'That's Carol's car'. So, I pulled over and we were waiting to see which store you came out of. Getting some copying done?"

"It is a surprise seeing the two of you here," Carol said, trying to sound pleasantly surprised. "What are you doing in Manchester?"

"We were on our way to a flower shop down the street," said Harriet. "A woman I know owns and operates it. We thought, Margaret and I, that we would get some flowers and drop them off at the hospital for Tina. We didn't want to order them over the phone. That is so impersonal. So, Margaret and I were on our way to pick up some flowers, drop them off at the hospital, and then maybe a light lunch. Why don't you join us?"

Harriet had suggested it with high enthusiasm, but inside, Carol was cringing. This was the last thing she wanted—to be seen coming from a copy center and then saddled with Harriet and Margaret for the afternoon and to be under their scrutiny.

"Sounds like a great idea!" Carol said.

8

Chalifour's Flowers was on Elm Street. Carol had never been there, and she found it a delightful shop despite her situation. It was a known fact that a person always felt better in a flower store. On entering the shop, the three women were hit with that flower store aroma—a combination of roses, peonies, lavender, carnations, and tulips. All these fragrances melded together to make that intoxicating floral odor that lifts the spirit and enriches the soul while giving one the sense of being outdoors.

Carol breathed in deep.

She did not know why she agreed to go with Harriet and Margaret. Perhaps, she thought, it was the normal thing to do and right now she needed, more than ever, to act normal. She did not want to look as if she had something to hide or had a big secret or had done some dastardly deed. There are some women who, when they suspect someone has a secret, feel they must know what it is, and some will go to great lengths to sniff it out. It is as if they must know. Most do not know why they must know, but they do. Carol was not sure Margaret and Harriet were those types of women, but she could not take that chance. She left her craft case containing her charts in the trunk of her car. It may have looked suspicious, but if she carried them around, the last thing she needed was to have the other two ask to see what she had, or worse, to look into the case. The three women had rode together in Harriet's car to the flower shop.

In the flower shop, Harriet was greeted by the owner, and Harriet explained why they were there—they wished to send flowers to a friend in the hospital. The owner, a very pleasant woman about fifty years of age, donned a concerned look.

"Is it terribly serious?" she asked Harriet.

"Oh, yes, poor dear. She fell in her own home and struck her head on the tiled floor. She cracked her head open and now she is in a coma."

The shop owner brought her fingers to her mouth. "My, my, that is just dreadful. You know, most accidents happen in the home. Did she fall in the bathroom? Most accidents at home occur in the bathroom."

"No," Harriet said, shaking her head. "It was in the kitchen—wasn't it?" Harriet asked turning to her friends. Both Margaret and Carol shrugged. "We're not sure where it happened, but I don't think she fell in the bathroom. It may have been the kitchen."

"I don't think the police detective said where exactly Tina fell," Carol said. "I remember him saying she fell on a tile floor. It could have been the kitchen."

Carol felt she had to be attentive and listen with a concerned countenance. At one point she saw Margaret watching her closely.

"Is she a very close friend?" the florist asked.

"We've known her for several years," Harriet said. "She's in our cross-stitch group."

"Oh, you belong to a cross-stitch group."

"Yes," said Harriet turning to Carol and Margaret. "We are all in the group."

The shop owner showed them a variety of get-well arrangements.

"This one looks like your cross-stitch," Harriet said to Carol.

At the words 'your cross-stitch', Carol tensed up, until she realized that Harriet meant the Flowers in a Vase cross-stitch.

Carol looked at the arrangement. "Yes, it does," she said, feigning delight. "It looks just like it."

"No, it doesn't," Margaret said, plainly. "It doesn't have any goldenrods and the carnations are a different color."

Margaret did not say much, but when she did it was usually surprising. She certainly had a good memory, Carol thought. Even Carol missed these details, and it was her cross-stitch.

"I could put in some goldenrods," the owner said. "No extra charge," she added.

It was a lovely arrangement that came to $35.98 plus tax. Harriet put it on her credit card, but Carol insisted on paying for her share right away. She gave Harriet ten dollars.

There were a few floral cards from which to choose. They picked one.

"Carol, would you like to fill out the card?" Harriet asked. "Just a short get-well message and all our names. Don't forget Amanda."

"Surely," Carol said. She picked up a pen and was preparing to write.

"Carol, dear, your hand is shaking," Harriet said as Carol held the pen. "Is something wrong?"

Carol tried to get her hand to stop trembling. "No... I was just thinking of poor Tina, in the hospital. It is all so upsetting."

"Here," Harriet said, taking the pen from Carol. "Allow me to do it."

In Harriet's car, Margaret sat in the passenger seat holding the arrangement, and Carol sat in the back seat.

The Catholic Medical Center was on McGregor Street. It was a large complex, but fortunately, there was free valet parking. The trio finally reached the main desk and inquired about Tina DeLuca.

They were informed that Tina DeLuca was in the Intensive Care Unit. No, visitors were not allowed in the room, unless they were relatives. No, the woman at the desk did not know when Tina could receive guests. That would be up to the doctor. I'm sorry, but flowers are not allowed in the ICU.

The women looked crestfallen.

"I suppose we should have called first," Harriet said.

"That is always best," the woman at the counter said. "You could send balloons or a plush toy. We have a very nice gift shop here."

"We already bought the flowers," Margaret said to her. "They were forty dollars."

"I'm sorry," the receptionist said. "There is nothing I can do."

The three women turned from the desk, dejected.

"Well, what now? What do we do with these flowers?" Carol said.

"We will leave them at Tina's house," Harriet said. "At least Vincent will know we are thinking of her."

They thought this was a good idea.

"Has anyone called Vincent?" Carol asked.

"Amanda said she wanted to, but I told her it was best to wait a few days," Harriet said.

Carol smiled. She had also told Amanda the same thing. It was just like Amanda to ask for a second opinion.

Harriet said, "Well, let's go to lunch. My treat."

Margaret voiced her approval, which was followed by deciding on a place to eat.

They ate at a diner close to the Merrimack River. Harriet suggested they bring in the flowers and set them on the table to enjoy. The food was good and reasonably priced. They ate in silence. Now and then Harriet tried to start a conversation, but Margaret and Carol weren't very talkative. After they ate, Harriet rose to go to the restroom.

"Do you want one of us to go with you?" Carol asked.

"Heavens, no," she said. "Stay and relax."

Carol sat rather uncomfortably with Margaret. She could not remember the two of them ever being alone together. Margaret was pretty closed-mouthed. Just as well. Carol did not want to talk.

"Were you copying some charts?"

"I beg your pardon?" Carol said. She wasn't ready for this, and Margaret seemed to blurt it out.

"Did you go to the copy store to copy cross-stitch charts?"

"Why do you think I was copying charts?"

"You were using one of your craft cases. You only use those for crafts."

"Oh, yes. Yes, I did. I was copying some old patterns."

"Which ones?"

"Oh, uhm, the Flowers in a Vase. You know, it's funny because we just mentioned it at the florist. I have an extra copy of the chart—would you like one?"

"That would be nice. Thank you."

"Think nothing of it."

"Maybe you could bring it to the next meeting."

"I will."

"What about the last project you were working on—Smith Falls?"

"Smith Falls?"

"Yes, the old-fashioned town with the gazebo—or is it a bandstand?"

This woman had some memory, Carol thought to herself.

"Tina asked for a copy of that pattern," Margaret said. "Were you making her a copy of the chart?"

"Yes, I was making her a copy. I am looking forward to giving it to her when she recovers."

"That is a kind gesture," Margaret said.

"It is nothing."

"No, no, it means you are thinking of Tina, and that is kind."

The uncomfortable silence returned. Carol looked to the washroom door, anticipating Harriet's return.

"Why did you come all the way into Manchester to do your copying?" Margaret asked.

"What was that?"

"Why come to Manchester to do your copying? There are places in Bedford where you could go. One is close to your house."

"Yes," said Carol nodding and grasping for an answer. "Yes, there is. Oh, look, here comes Harriet."

Harriet told Carol that she and Margaret would drop off the flowers at Tina's house.

"Would you care to come with us?" she asked.

"Normally I would love to join you, but I did not plan to be away this long, and I have somewhere to be. Thanks for lunch."

They dropped Carol off where she had left her car. She got her craft case out of the trunk, put it on the seat next to her, and drove home.

Once inside her house, she put her craft case back in the closet. Carol was tired. She was tired of thinking of everything that had occurred and the dilemma she faced. She was tired of trying not to get caught in a lie, and worrying about every word that came out of her mouth. She was tired of Margaret's questions. If Carol did not know better, she suspected that Margaret thought something was up.

Carol was scheduled for an afternoon shift at Crafty Business. She went in, hoping the job would help her keep her mind off her troubles. It didn't, of course.

The next few days Carol did everything but work on her cross-stitch. She felt afraid to even look at it. Somehow, the cross-stitch was the cause of her terrible predicament. How was this possible? She thought about her journey to Smith

Falls. How could anything so wonderful as Smith Falls have anything to do with Tina's tragic accident?

Just when Carol thought she couldn't feel any worse, Amanda called.

"Hello, Amanda."

"I heard you, Harriet, and Margaret went out to lunch." Amanda sounded a bit snarky. "I can't believe you would purposely leave me out."

"Amanda—"

"And the three of you picked out flowers for Tina."

"Amanda—"

"And you all went to the hospital—without me?"

"Listen to me, Amanda, listen to me. I ran into Margaret and Harriet quite by accident. They decided to move on the flowers, and they were going to the hospital. When we bumped into each other in Manchester—"

"What were you doing in Manchester?"

"Amanda, try to focus—"

"What about your lunch date?"

"It wasn't a date; it was a spur-of-the-moment thing."

"I feel so left out, Carol. Do you know how that feels? I thought you all were my friends. Friends consider one another. Friends love one another. You could have called me. I would have liked to have been there."

"Amanda—you're right. One of us should have called you. We didn't exclude you deliberately, but we could have put out an effort to get in touch with you. I apologize."

"Thank you, Carol. That means a lot to me."

"Don't mention it."

"I was talking with the others—Margaret and Harriet—and they suggested the four of us get together soon. Not to cross-stitch but just to talk and be together. We thought next Saturday would be good. Is Saturday good for you?"

"Perfect."

"We'll meet at The Friendly Toast at nine o'clock for breakfast."

"Sounds good."

"And don't worry, Carol. I won't call and remind you."

For the first time in days, Carol felt a touch of humanity. For just a minute she had gotten out of herself and made another person feel good, and it did not take as much effort as she thought it might. Carol believed she was a good person. She had goodness in her. Her actions with Tina were not her finer moments. She was sorry and wished it had never happened. Would telling everyone the truth be of any help to Tina at all?

The very next day Carol felt different. She felt good. The itch to cross-stitch—as Amanda was so fond of saying—started to pull at her. Deep down Carol knew she could not totally abandon Smith Falls. She promised herself that she would only work on it in private, and in her own home.

As soon as Carol started back on the cross-stitch, it felt right. There was something almost magical about this project. Even though it seemed like the cross-stitch led to a tragedy, Carol was determined that she would not allow that to happen again.

Day after day Smith Falls took on more detail. Carol's stitching was fleshing out the town. There were more shops, more activities, and more people. There was one character in particular that intrigued her, a man in a high hat and carrying a walking stick. Carol was not certain, but she knew he was important.

She never ceased to be amazed at how the quality of her work constantly improved. Her floss never tangled, and her stitches were consistent and true. It is not that the work was effortless, indeed, Carol felt she had never put more effort into a project. She could not deny that she felt invigorated by this project, but she was also aware that the work could just as well drain her. After working on the project for hours she would hit a wall and could not do one more stitch. That was how she felt now, her fingers would not obey, and her eyes grew so heavy she could not keep them open. The feeling was familiar, as if she had experienced it before.

9

To Carol, the feeling was familiar. She had experienced it before—the feeling of the sun on her face. It was warm, refreshing, and revitalizing. The air was brisk and invigorating. She breathed it in deeply. Carol raised her parasol. A light breeze caressed her face like a gentle touch of a lover. A horse-drawn carriage went by. The clip-clop cadence was rhythmical and steady like a metronome. Even her hearing was enhanced. She perceived each sound clearly—a fountain tinkled, leaves rustled, and a voice called her name.

In the very air there existed a perceived calmness, a peace like she had never known. Carol felt she would have been content just to sit on a park bench and be still, observing, and being a part of everything around her. Here was a place to slow down, to divest herself of worry and sadness. Carol felt such comfort and joy welling up inside her, and she felt a single tear run down her cheek. It was a tear derived from pure joy, pure love, pure being. She dabbed it dry with a gloved hand. This is true happiness, she thought. This is what happiness feels like.

Some of that happiness came from an indescribable sense of being and belonging. Somehow the town and everything in it was connected to everything and each other. That included Carol as well. She was a part of it all. It was as if Smith Falls was tied together by a single thread that ran through everything. It was a fixity, a union like Carol had never known or even conceived. She belonged here.

Carol looked down the street. Mr. Robert C. Crawford and his fiancé, Miss Penelope Hope were walking towards her. They greeted her pleasantly.

"Good day, Caroline," he said, giving a small tip of his hat.

"Caroline, it is so wonderful to see you again," Miss Hope said.

"Good day to you both," Carol said, smiling. She could not help but smile. It was this place. She liked it here. It gave her a sense of well-being that she had not experienced in her entire life.

"It is a lovely day, don't you think, Caroline?" Penelope Hope said.

"Yes, it is lovely."

"A very lovely day," Robert Crawford said.

"It is the kind of day where one can forget all their troubles, all their sorrow," Penelope said, gently, as she laid a gloved hand reassuringly on Carol's hand. "Be at peace, dear Caroline. There is nothing to harm you here."

"Nothing?"

"You are perfectly safe with us, Caroline," Crawford said, with soothing reassurance.

"Am I?"

"Of course, you are, Caroline, dear. We are your friends," Penelope said. "You are entirely safe in Smith Falls."

"Yes, I am," Carol said with conviction.

"What a grand day it is," Crawford said, casting a glance around them.

Penelope's face broke out in a wide grin, displaying white, even teeth. "And today is a special day. Do you know why?" she asked Carol. "Because today you are going to meet Mr. Pennington."

"Who?"

"Mr. Walter Pennington. Oh, Caroline, you are just going to adore him, I know you are. I am certain the two of you will get along famously."

"Well, who is he?"

"Who is he?" Crawford repeated as if it were a silly question.

"Caroline, Walter Pennington is a close personal friend of ours and is known throughout all of Smith Falls," Penelope said.

"He has a very good reputation," Crawford chimed in. "A stellar reputation."

"As what?"

"As a splendid chap, that's what," he said. "A most excellent chap. I know him all to pieces."

Robert and Penelope appeared so happy it was contagious. Carol could not help but smile and laugh and be happy as well. Any concern or fear she may have had, now all disappeared. When she was in Smith Falls, she did not think about any other place.

"When will I meet him, the well-known Mr. Walter Pennington?"

"Today! Very soon now," Penelope said. "He is known to walk this way. Oh, Caroline, I do envy you. Walter Pennington is such a fine gentleman, so dashing, and quite handsome too."

"I believe that is Walter Pennington coming this way now," Robert Crawford said, looking down the street.

The two women followed his gaze. They saw a tall man, made to look even taller by his high hat which was grey with a dark band. He dressed impeccably in a dark coat with large lapels and tailored at the waist. He wore an ivory vest, a white shirt, and a dark tie. He had baby blue trousers with white vertical stripes and polished black boots. In his right hand, he carried a black walking stick with a silver head.

The trio stepped forward to meet the debonair Mr. Walter Pennington.

"Good day, Walter," Robert called out and as they met the two men shook hands.

"Good day, Robert," said Walter Pennington. "Isn't it a glorious day?

"It certainly is," said Robert. "Walter, you remember my fiancé, of course, Miss Penelope Hope.

"Of course," he said smiling. He tipped his hat, took her outstretched hand, and bowed over it. "How could I forget such a charming and beautiful young lady? You are a lucky man, Robert."

Penelope drank in his compliments with a smile. "Good day, Mr. Pennington."

Pennington turned to Carol, and said, "But I am certain I have not had the extreme pleasure of meeting this fine woman."

Carol felt herself blush.

"Where are my manners?" Robert said. "May I present our friend, Miss Caroline Crane. Caroline, this is Mr. Walter Pennington."

Pennington reached out and took Carol's hand. "Charmed, I am sure. Caroline; what a lovely name. How does that old verse go? Caroline, Caroline …. something, something… oh, I'll remember it."

"How do you do, Mr. Pennington," she said. "It is a pleasure to meet you."

"The pleasure is mine, I am sure," he said, looking deep into her eyes.

Carol flushed. She could not remember a time—if ever—a man met her eyes like this. She felt his interest in her—she mattered. She felt love and acceptance. Perhaps not romantic love, but love, nonetheless. This place, she knew, was where she wanted to be.

"Shall we go for a stroll?" Robert Crawford said.

"That is an excellent idea," Walter Pennington said. He offered his arm to Carol, and she took it.

Carol felt on top of the world. Her step was lighter, as was her heart. They walked down the street of shops she had seen on her previous visit. When they passed the florists, Carol broke off from Pennington and motioned Penelope to follow her. The two women went into the florist and emerged minutes later. Each faced their escort and placed a white carnation in the buttonhole of the men's coat. The boutonnieres looked so bright against their dark clothes.

"There," Carol said to Pennington, "now you are perfect."

As they approached the men's haberdashery, they slowed and looked in the window. In the window was a neat display of hats, ties, handkerchiefs, and waistcoats or vests.

"I've been of the mind to get a new hat," Crawford said to Penelope. "Let's have a look, shall we?"

Pennington opened the door and held it open for all of them to pass through.

In the haberdashery were many shelves, some that went up almost to the ceiling. There were mahogany hutches and drawers, and cubby storage units of every size. They all gave the store a distinctive woody odor.

A very well-dressed, short balding man came out from behind the counter to greet his customers and asked if he could show them anything.

Crawford gave the man his hat size and asked to see a selection of hats. While the owner went to collect a selection of hats, the ladies were offered a seat on a pair of matching Victorian Slipper chairs.

Crawford tried on a variety of top hats, bowlers, wide awakes, and homburgs, all with subtle shades and hatbands. It was a delightful time for all of them, as Crawford and Pennington ceaselessly made clever comments and humorous observations, some at Crawford's expense. He accepted them good-naturedly.

Robert Crawford could not decide on any of the hats he tried on.

"Do you know what I truly need," he said. "I need a hat for Lady Wyndemere's garden party."

"Of course, the garden party," said Penelope. "I had almost forgotten about it."

Robert Crawford settled on a Straw Boater's Hat with a large black band with a narrow red band in the center of it. He gave the haberdasher his card and told him to deliver the hat to his home.

Once on the pavement again, Penelope said with a start, "Lady Wyndemere's garden party! We haven't told Caroline about the garden party."

"Oh, how gauche!" Robert uttered.

"There is a remedy," Walter said.

"Of course. Oh, Caroline, please, forgive us, and tell us you will come," Penelope said.

"I would love to come."

Everyone smiled and Walter said, "There, another tragedy averted."

"The four of us at a garden party," said Penelope, "won't that be wonderful!"

The four friends walked down the street until the pavement ended and a wide dirt path lay before them. They left the town behind and entered a more rural setting. There were more leafy and evergreen trees, and long grass bordered the dirt road. It was different than being in town, but still, Carol found it wonderful.

They eventually came to a stream or a small river whose grass banks slope gently to the water's edge. Two youths paddled by in a red canoe. They raised their paddles in a greeting to the two couples on shore.

The four of them sat on the grassy bank in the shade of a large willow tree that swayed from the breeze. They sat in silence for a long time, taking in the peaceful setting and enjoying each other's company.

"What body of water is that?" Carol asked.

"Hutton Creek," Robert Crawford said. "I used to fish and swim in it when I was a boy."

"Just a cane pole, a hook, and some worms," Walter said. "I remember tying together logs into a raft and poling down the creek."

Carol ruminated that Smith Falls had always been like this. It was constant, unchanging. It was a place caught in a wonderful time. She was happy here and knew she would be happy to spend the rest of her life here.

Before long, Robert and Penelope stood up and announced they were going for a short walk.

Carol and Walter watched them walk off hand-in-hand.

"Young love," Walter said.

"I find it refreshing and gives me hope for the future," Carol said.

"I am glad you feel that way, Caroline. Everyone deserves to be happy. Are you happy?"

"I am when I am here. I am now… here with you."

He took her by the hand. "If I could remove all your past pain and suffering, all your worry and woe, I would do it. Do you believe that?"

"Yes."

"I only wish for you to be happy," he said. "Do you believe that?"

"Yes," she said.

He brought her hand to his lips, pulled back her glove, and kissed the back of her hand.

She was happy. She was overflowing with joy.

Subsequently, Robert and Penelope returned.

"We should be getting back, I suppose," Robert said. Penelope nodded in agreement.

A short walk brought the four of them back to Smith Falls. At the bandstand, Robert and Penelope wished their friends a good day and went on their way.

"So, I hope you will do me the honor of allowing me to escort you to Lady Wyndemere's garden party."

"Of course. I am looking forward to it."

"And I am looking forward to introducing you to Lady Wyndemere. You will like her, and I am certain she will like you."

"I look forward to meeting Lady Wyndemere."

"I just recalled that old verse," he said, touching his temple.

"*Caroline, Caroline,*
True beauty be thine,
Caroline, Caroline,
Say you'll be mine."

"Oh, my," she said, and there was such a rush of blood to her head, that she thought she might swoon. "I do not believe I have ever heard that. Who is the poet?"

A slight smile touched his lips. "Me," he said, and with a tip of his hat, he bid her good day and said he would be counting the days until he saw her again.

Carol could barely contain herself. Her heart raced. Part of her wanted to be ravished by him, right then and there. She felt dizzy and had to hold on to the rail of the bandstand to keep from falling.

She watched him walk down the street, jauntily, swinging his stick. Her heart pounded and she wanted him to turn around and look at her. He didn't though. It didn't matter to Carol. No man had ever recited poetry to her, let alone written a poem for her. The two of them had an almost instant attraction. If one thing was certain, she knew she was in love with Mr. Walter Pennington, and he was in love with her. But they had only just met. How was this possible? She believed almost anything was possible in Smith Falls.

Carol turned as she became aware of the sound of pounding. She knew it was not the pounding of her heart. This was different. It was something outside herself. The pounding grew louder. She wondered if there was some construction going on in Smith Falls. The pounding got louder and louder. Carol looked around her, wondering from which direction the pounding originated. It got so loud she raised her hands to her ears to deafen the sound. She closed her eyes and hoped the pounding would stop.

10

Carol awoke to the sound of someone pounding on her front door. She rose from the sofa and stood on shaky legs. After taking a moment to steady herself, she made her way to the door and opened it. Amanda was standing there with an incredible look of worry and horror on her face.

"Carol! Oh, thank goodness! We were afraid something happened to you!"

"We?"

Amanda motioned to Margaret and Harriet who were sitting in Harriet's car. At Amanda's signal, they got out and approached the house.

"Did you really need to pound on my door like that?" Carol asked, perturbed. "Couldn't you just call?"

"Carol, I did call—four times. You didn't answer."

By now Margaret and Harriet were at the door.

"Come on in everyone, if you want to," Carol said, still trying to shake off her disorientation.

"Carol, we were worried," Harriet said.

"You were late," Margaret added with less concern.

"Late for what?" Carol asked.

"The Friendly Toast, nine o'clock, remember?" Amanda said.

"What time is it now?"

"It's after ten," Margaret said.

"Honey," Harriet spoke lovingly, "We waited and called, and waited and called. After what happened to Tina, we got worried about you. Finally, we decided to come here and see if you were all right."

"I must have fallen asleep," Carol said. "I think I left my phone in my purse on vibrate."

"We were so worried," Amanda said.

"Why didn't you give me a reminder call yesterday?" Carol said to Amanda.

"Are you kidding me?" Amanda said.

"We haven't eaten," Margaret said, moodily.

Margaret saw Carol's cross-stitch and walked over to it. "Were you working on this when you fell asleep?"

"Yes... no... I don't know. Why?"

Margaret didn't answer.

"Carol, are you all right?" Harriet asked, her face tinged with worry.

"Yes, I'm fine."

"Have you been drinking?"

"No. I don't think so. No. I haven't had a drink in days."

The three women looked at one another with a look that they had worried for nothing, and their concern was not appreciated.

"What do we do now?" said Margaret. "I'm hungry."

They all looked at Carol as if to say, *this is your fault, do you have any ideas?*

Carol picked up on this and said, "Let me change and I'll take you all to breakfast at a place I know."

The four of them ended up at the IHOP on River Road. Inside they sat in a cozy booth with Harriet and Margaret on one side, and Carol and Amanda on the other. After they ordered they sat in an uncomfortable silence for several minutes.

"We took those flowers over to Tina's house," Harriet said. "We knocked, but no one seemed at home, so we left them on the porch by the door. Vincent hasn't called to acknowledge them. I'm sure he has other things on his mind."

"Maybe he doesn't know our phone numbers," Amanda said.

"Tina has our numbers and addresses in her book," said Margaret. "That is how that detective got our addresses."

"Did you put my name on the card?" Amanda asked.

"Of course, we did. Why wouldn't we?" Harriet said.

"Well, I wasn't with you when you bought them," said Amanda, petulantly.

"That is enough of that, Amanda," Margaret said.

"Has anyone heard back from that Det. Jarmon?" Carol said.

They all looked at her.

Their coffees came. Milk and sugar were added. Spoons clink in cups. Sips were taken.

"Why should we hear from Jarmon again?" Harriet asked.

Carol shrugged.

"It was strange, Tina having that accident," Margaret said.

"Strange how?" Carol asked.

"Tina always seemed graceful," Amanda said. "It wasn't like her to have such a slip and fall. She's been in that house for years and never fell on that floor."

"As far as we know," said Carol. "Tina wasn't the type to admit to something like that."

"What do you mean?" Amanda said.

"Just what you said. Tina had a reputation for being graceful. I don't think she would readily admit to being clumsy."

The women nodded. Tina was their friend, but there was no point in making out she was better than she was. They all knew Tina's good qualities as well as her bad.

"Besides, that floor was slippery," insisted Carol. "I almost slipped and fell." She looked at Harriet.

"So did I," Harriet said.

"Still, it wasn't like Tina," Margaret insisted.

"Well, what do you think happened," Carol asked Margaret. As soon as she said these words, she wished she hadn't. Best to let it go. No good would come from prolonging this conversation. Best to change the subject, but before she could, Margaret answered her.

"Tina could have been arguing with someone and things got violent," Margaret proposed. "It may have been a home invasion."

They all looked at her with shock.

"But Jarmon would have known that; don't you think?" Harriet said.

"How would he have known?" Margaret asked.

"There would have been something stolen, wouldn't there?" Carol said.

"Not necessarily," Harriet said.

Amanda wanted to contribute to this. "Maybe if someone broke in, they struggled with Tina, she fell and struck her head, and the person panicked and fled before stealing anything. Don't you think that's possible, Carol?"

"What?"

"Whoever struggled with Tina panicked after she fell and hit her head. Might that be what happened?"

"I guess," Carol said, reluctantly.

"If that's the case," said Harriet, "whoever it could have been, was criminal for not calling the police or ambulance."

"It was evil," Margaret said.

"Evil?" Carol said.

"It was evil," Margaret repeated.

"They could have made an anonymous call to the police," Amanda said.

"Maybe they were afraid the police would trace the number," Carol said. Why was she prolonging this? She was determined not to say anymore.

"They could have called from a payphone," Harriet said.

"There aren't any pay phones anymore," Amanda said. "Very few, at any rate."

"I guess I'm showing my age," Harriet said.

"Has anyone thought of Vincent?" Amanda said.

"What about him?" asked Harriet.

"Maybe Vincent came home earlier than he said to the police. Maybe he came home early, and he and Tina got into an argument, and he caused her to fall. He either left and came back, or he waited until the usual hour he came home to phone the police."

"Why would he have waited?" Margaret asked Amanda.

Amanda thought a moment. "If Vincent was responsible for Tina's accident and did not wish to come under suspicion, then he needed to create a false time frame from the time we left, or rather when Carol left until he came home at his regular time. Thereby there is a window of opportunity for a third party to have attacked Tina. Maybe Vincent wanted to lead Jarmon to suspect someone else attacked Tina."

"But if... no, when Tina comes out of her coma, she would be able to say that it was Vincent who attacked her," Harriet said.

"What if Vincent doesn't plan to have Tina come out of her coma?" Amanda said nefariously.

"How would he do that?" Harriet asked.

Amanda thought. "Tina's in the hospital. Maybe he plans on unplugging the machine Tina is on."

"Is Tina on a machine?" Margaret asked.

"She must be," said Harriet.

"What—?" began Margaret but was cut off.

"Maybe no one attacked Tina," Carol could not help but speak up. "Maybe Tina simply slipped and fell. End of story. Let's stop speculating and making out like Vincent is a killer."

The table went completely silent but all of them could not help but consider all that was said.

Just then, their waitress arrived with their food order and there ensued a bit of confusion about their orders.

Thank God, thought Carol. Now they have something else to occupy their mouths.

Across the table, she saw Margaret and Harriet silently say grace before they ate. Coffee cups were refilled, and the food looked scrumptious. Carol, however, did not have much of an appetite and picked at her food slowly. She asked if anyone wanted her toast and Margaret scooped it up quickly before anyone else could.

"We haven't spoken about getting together for our next cross-stitch session," Harriet said, seemingly out of nowhere. The table had been quiet for some time.

They all looked at her as if she had said a dirty word.

"I never thought we would stop meeting for cross-stitch out of some loyalty to Tina," she said. "It was certainly awful what happened, but it was an accident, and I see no reason why we should stop meeting regularly."

"Don't you think it is disrespectful to Tina," Amanda whispered.

"No," Harriet said clearly. "In fact, it is more important now to meet. It is a way of showing support for each other and to keep Tina in our thoughts. We should not let this terrible accident keep us from getting together and doing what we love."

They were all in agreement with Harriet, and since it was her turn, Harriet would host the next cross-stitch session at her home.

Amanda leaned over and whispered to Carol, "Would you like me to give you a reminder call?"

"That would be very nice of you."

The next few days Carol worked on her Smith Falls cross-stitch. She was eager to return to the town—eager to see her new friend, but she was not certain how to return. There seemed to be no known way to do that except to work on the cross-stitch. Even then, it never seemed to happen right away or when she wanted it to happen. Her two visits to Smith Falls happened seemingly by chance. There was no incantation, or prayer, or formula. Both times she went to Smith Falls were not on the same day of the week, or a month with an R in it, or when Venus and Mars were aligned. All she could do was work on the project and wait for it to happen.

One day, Carol got it in her head to return to Malum Crafts. She did not know what the point of going back would be. After all, what would she say? What would she tell them? If Carol told them she had visited Smith Falls, would they believe her? Would they think her crazy? She did not care. Carol wanted some answers and was determined to get them.

It took her almost an hour to find the original directions to Malum Crafts.

When she first drove to the craft store, Carol got lost. She seemed to find it quite by accident, and one would think she could easily find her way back. The store could not be found on Google or anywhere on the internet. She berated herself for not putting it in her GPS.

Carol had no more luck finding the place the second time—no more luck, no less. After what felt like traveling in circles for hours, there it was. To be truthful, it looked less eerie in the daylight compared to night, then again, everything must be like that.

She parked close by and looked about. No one seemed to be around. Trying the door, she found it locked. She knocked. There was no response. Carol looked about again. Trees lined both sides of the road and one could not see far. There were junipers, hemlock, cedar, and spruce. There were wildflowers such as red columbine, purple coneflower, and Virginia bluebell.

Carol walked about slowly, not venturing far from her car. Clouds blocked out the sun and wind tossed about the branches of trees. Carol looked up. Looks like rain, she thought. She turned back to her car.

"Yup!"

The voice appeared to come from nowhere, and Carol jumped at the sound of it. She turned around and a man stood twenty feet from her. She was certain he was not standing there before she turned around, nor did she see anyone approach.

The man stood tall and looked like a custodian or gardener from the way he was dressed. His clothes were ill-fitting and dirty. His long coat reached to his knees. He wore dirty rubber boots and carried an old shovel on his shoulder. His appearance made Carol think of a crazy gravedigger from a bad horror movie.

His looks and manner left Carol very uncomfortable, and she should have run to her car, but she was so struck by his appearance that she could not move.

The man's face was shadowed by a wide-brimmed hat. His eyes were mere slits, his beak-shaped nose was long and fleshless. He had a long gaunt face and a wide lipless mouth. His long hair looked greasy and was streaked with gray.

"You want something?" he asked. His voice was low and gruff.

Carol could not find her voice but managed to point to the store.

The man looked at the store and then back to Carol.

"Store's closed."

Carol nodded and turned to her car. She walked over to it quickly, got in, and locked the doors. She started the engine. The man was at her window looking in. Carol stifled the desire to scream.

"Store is open tomorrow," he said.

She put the car in gear and hurriedly drove away.

11

Carol arrived home somewhat shaken. There was something very strange about that store. She suspected it before, but now she was certain of it. In one way she wished she had never gone there, and Tina's accident would never have happened. But she knew that was ridiculous. If she had not gone to Malum Crafts, Carol would never have gone to Smith Falls. It was indeed a dilemma that she could not reason through.

Once home again, she went into her closet and took out the craft bag that contained the Smith Falls cross-stitch. Unzipping the case, she removed the cross-stitch and set it on her bed. She sat looking at it, and strangely she felt it looked back at her. It gave her a feeling that she could not readily describe. That cross-stitch, she thought—what kind of magic or power did it possess? Smith Falls was not a dream, and she was not insane, she concluded. Carol knew she had been there and saw the town. She had walked and talked with people.

After her first visit, Carol had suspected Smith Falls was a figment of her imagination stirred by the cross-stitch scene. Perhaps she wanted or needed a place like that in which to retreat, a place in which she could find solace and comfort from this world. In this world, everything seemed to be falling around her ears. In Smith Falls there was peace—peace and a sense of belonging.

But how was Smith Falls connected to the cross-stitch? Was it merely a reflection of the cross-stitch? If she cut out part of the bandstand, would that be reflected in her next visit there? Would she find the bandstand under construction, or find it in the middle of being repaired for some reason? Oh, my! What if she cut out a character like Mr. Walter Pennington? Would she return to find him deathly ill, or dead, or missing? Did her work on the cross-stitch affect Smith Falls and the people who lived there? And where did they live? Is it part of the past, or some other world, some other dimension? Do they know of Carol's world? Can they cross over to Bedford, New Hampshire?

Was the cross-stitch merely a gateway to Smith Falls? Did the town exist independently from the cross-stitch? It must, for, on her last visit, Carol and the others sat by a creek. There is no creek on the cross-stitch. That must mean there is an entire world waiting there. That world does not depend on what Carol cross-stitches. Or does it?

So many questions she could not answer. So many possibilities. The entire matter made her head spin. There were so many things about it she did not know.

One thing she did know—she liked being in Smith Falls. Carol felt welcomed and loved there. She could not wait to go back.

Going into the kitchen she poured herself a drink. Thus fortified, Carol went into the spare bedroom and began to clear it of all the collection of things she and Gary had gathered in their time together. There was the antique folding rocker she bought with the intention of stripping it down, refinishing it, and reupholstering it. She even bought the material, but that was as far as she got. There was quite a collection of unfinished projects—not all of them hers. There was an assortment of pictures that were never hung or even framed, clothes that were never worn, and books that were never read. She wondered if Gary would want them.

It was quite a job, and it took her hours before the room was cleared, and stored those things in the basement, which too was a mess. This room would now be her cross-stitch room and Smith Falls would never leave this room. She brought in a nice comfortable chair to sit in while she stitched and set up an old stereo so she could listen to nice relaxing music while she worked. She put an end table next to her chair, and upon the table, Carol set her OttLite to stitch by. Once she had everything all set up for cross-stitching, Carol wondered why she had never set up a room for her cross-stitching sooner. She supposed it was because up until now she had not had to take her stitching too seriously. She could stitch while she and Gary watched TV or just while sitting around the house. Now she had a room to work on Smith Falls. If someone were visiting, she would simply close the door to the room. Maybe she could lock it. By the time the room was done and ready for her to get some serious stitching done, it was very late, and she had to go to bed.

The next day was a busy one for Carol. She had to work the breakfast shift at the Golden Griddle, and then it was over to Crafty Business till 6:00. She was eager to get home.

This was the first day Carol worked on the cross-stitch in her new cross-stitch room. She played some Yo-Yo Ma and some Jesse Cook and she felt she was in heaven.

The next day Carol received a call from Amanda and Carol was certain she had forgotten a meeting or lunch date or something. But it was none of those mundane or ordinary things. To Carol it was shocking.

"Carol, great news!" Amanda began, excitedly. "This is such a surprise! And I called you before any of the others!"

"What is it, Amanda? What is so great?"

"It's Tina!"

"What about Tina?" Carol said, trying to keep her voice from trembling.

"She opened her eyes, today!"

"She what?"

"She opened her eyes! Isn't that great?"

"Did Tina say anything? Did she speak?"

"Why, no, she didn't. At least I don't think so, but she opened her eyes for a few seconds. Her eyes fluttered open, then they fluttered close."

"How do you know—"

"I called Tina's husband, Vincent, today and he told me."

"You called Vincent?"

"Yes, I just wanted to make sure he knew those flowers were from me, as well."

"We put your name on the card, Amanda."

"I know, I just wanted to be sure he knew it."

"What exactly did Vincent say?" Carol asked, trying not to sound too eager. She chewed nervously on the nail of her left index finger.

"Vincent told me he had just returned home from the hospital because they called him that Tina had an eye flutter."

"Wait a minute, did she open her eyes, or did they just flutter open?"

"I don't know. It's the same thing, isn't it? Tina opened her eyes!

"But she didn't say anything?"

"No, but it's something. It's an improvement. Maybe Tina will wake up soon."

"Is that the opinion of her doctor?"

"They all told Vincent not to get his hopes up."

"Then why do you have your hopes up? And then you call me to get my hopes up."

"Carol, this is important, and I thought you would want to know."

"Well, certainly I want to know, Amanda. It is good news. Are you going to call Harriet and Margaret?"

"Yes, I was."

"Thanks, Amanda. Thanks for calling. I think it's great news."

"It is, isn't it? Do you want to hear what else?" Amanda said this like a little girl with a secret.

"Sure, what do you have?"

"When I was talking to Vincent, he was at home. Right in the middle of our conversation, I heard this woman's voice. I heard her say, "Vincent, are we going out tonight?" Just like that! He must have covered up the phone and told her to be quiet because I did not hear her speak again."

"What are you saying?"

"Isn't it obvious? Tina's in the hospital in a coma, and Vincent is bringing home some floozy. Isn't that awful!"

"Yes. Yes, it is."

By the time Carol hung up the phone, she was biting all her nails. If Tina was on the road to recovery, it could mean bad news for Carol. Bad news? If Tina were to relate what happened that day, Carol might end up in jail. Even if she was not charged with some crime, she could never show her face in Bedford. *That's the woman who left her friend to die, bleeding on the floor*, people would say as they pointed at her. Carol might not be able to live anywhere in New Hampshire. Surely this story would follow her around wherever she went.

She ran through a list of excuses about why she didn't help Tina after she struck her head on the floor. None of them sounded plausible, or reasonable. If she said she panicked and ran, it would make her look like a coward. No, you do not leave an injured person for any reason. Then again, she did not believe there was a law that forces a person to lend aid. Then again, Carol was partly responsible for Tina's fall. Most people would wonder why Carol simply did not call an ambulance.

It would be wrong to wish that Tina stayed in a coma forever. If and when Carol became a permanent resident of Smith Falls, then she would not care half as much if Tina came out of her coma and told everyone what happened. If the truth came out, it wouldn't touch Carol if she were safe in Smith Falls. No one in Smith Falls seemed aware of her past and no one ever would.

Carol did not sleep well that night. The thought of Tina recovering from her coma preyed on her mind. What should she do? What could she do? Perhaps some answer would come to her in the morning.

Carol rose the next morning knowing where she was going, but not knowing exactly why or what she would do when she got there. She had to work that day so her objective would wait.

After work, Carol got in her car and drove north on the 101 to Boynton Street, then to Main Street, and finally McGregor Street where she arrived at the Catholic Medical

Center. She did not use the valet parking but parked her car herself and walked to the main entrance of the hospital. Inside she inquired as to the condition of Tina DeLuca. She was told Tina's condition was stable and had been moved to a private room—4012, but no visitors outside of the family were allowed in her room. She thanked the woman at the desk and asked for directions to the gift shop. Carol walked away from the desk but did not go to the gift shop. Instead, she rode the elevator up to the Intensive Care Unit. Two other people rode the elevator with Carol, but she did not notice them. The people got off the elevator and left Carol by herself. Carol's pulse increased. She reached her floor and the doors opened. She gingerly stepped out of the elevator. The doors closed behind her. Carol stood there looking about. It was very quiet. Surprisingly no one appeared to be around. She saw no other visitors, no doctors, or nurses. Walking ever so gently she started to search for room 4012. Her footsteps sounded loud to her, and she was certain someone would hear her and demand to know what she was doing in the ICU. Someone walked down at the end of a long hall. They did not appear to see her. Carol found the room and stepped inside. My God, there she was. Carol barely recognized Tina. She was lying in a bed with her head wrapped in a wide bandage, and she had a few tubes coming out of her mouth and one in her nose. Carol stepped closer and despite never having seen Tina without makeup or being made up, she saw that it was indeed her. She looked so ordinary, so plain. Tina was unconscious but did not appear to be in any pain.

Any feelings of resentment she once had for Tina now dissolved away seeing her in this pitiful condition.

The room was eerily quiet save for the low hum of machines, and the sound of Tina's breathing. Carol looked at the machines with their lights and switches. She wondered which machine did what. What would happen, she thought, if one machine was turned off? What if two were turned off? How long could Tina live without these machines? Would an alarm sound if a machine was turned off? Carol stepped closer to the machines.

"Excuse me—what are you doing here?"

The voice was low but authoritative. For a brief instant, Carol thought it was Tina. No, it came from behind her.

Carol turned and standing at the door was a nurse. The woman's face showed stern consternation.

"Are you supposed to be here?" she asked Carol. "Did you sign in at the desk?"

All Carol could do was nod her head. The nurse gave her a suspicious look and was about to say something when Tina's husband, Vincent, came in. He was dark, tall, and rather handsome. He was still dressed in a business suit, and it looked as if he had worn it all day. His tie was loose, and his clothes rumpled.

They all looked questioningly at one another.

"Excuse me, Mr. DeLuca, do you know this woman?" the nurse asked him.

Vincent looked at Carol. Dawning recognition came over his face. They had only met twice and those times rather briefly.

"Yes," he said. "She is a friend of my wife."

They all spoke in a low voice, almost a whisper.

The nurse gave one last look of disapproval. "Visitations are limited to family members only."

"I understand," Vincent said.

The nurse gave Carol another glare and continued her rounds.

"I am surprised to find you here…," Vincent said, grasping for a name. "It's Karen, isn't it?"

"Carol."

"Oh, yes, that's right. What are you doing here, Carol?"

She flubbed for a response. Finally, she said, "Tina is my friend. I wanted to know how she was doing. I am concerned for her."

He regarded her as if he did not totally believe her. Vincent glanced from Carol to the machine she stood nearby.

He looked back at her and continued to stare at her as if he wished to make her feel uncomfortable. It worked.

"No change, then?" she said. "No improvement?"

"Very little, I'm afraid," he said, softening a bit.

"But she opened her eyes the other day! That's something!"

"The doctor said it may have been an involuntary reflex."

"And, of course, Tina hasn't spoken or said anything in her sleep."

"No—she hasn't said a word."

After a minute of uncomfortable silence, Carol said, "And how about you, Vincent, how are you holding up?"

He was a bit surprised by this. "You know, I'm coping."

"Yes, it must be very difficult for you. You must be lonely with Tina here, you not going out at all— No, wait, I think I saw you out on the town the other night. You were with someone. A young woman."

Vincent's face fell slack. He stared at Carol with cold dark eyes. He looked at the prone, still figure on the bed.

"Let's go into the hall," he said and motioned Carol out of the room.

They stood outside the room away from the door. "Would you care to repeat that, please?" he said, curtly.

Carol kept up her innocent tone. "I was just saying that, despite everything that has happened, it is good that you are getting out."

"I don't know where you thought you might have seen me, but I haven't been out, and I certainly was not with some young woman. I work, come here, and go home. That's all."

"I was certain that was you I saw."

"No, it wasn't me. Where was this?"

"You know what—you say it wasn't you, so let's let it go at that. Maybe I was wrong, and it wasn't you... with some young woman."

"Listen, Karen—"

"Carol."

"Carol, I don't know what you—"

"Did you get the flowers?"

"The what?"

"The flowers. Some of the ladies and I from the cross-stitch group bought flowers for Tina, but they don't allow flowers in
ICU, so two of the ladies took them to your house. Did you get them?"

"Yes, I believe so."

"I think they left them on your porch. They were in a vase. There were carnations, roses, and tulips. It was quite lovely. So, you got them?"

"Yes, I got them."

"Oh, good."

"I think it is time to go now, Carol."

She looked at her watch. "Why yes, it is. "

"Next time you should wait until the doctor says it is okay for Tina to have friends visit. Right now, she is limited to only relatives."

She nodded with a smile. "You know, Vincent, maybe you should get out a bit in the evenings. Treat yourself. You look like you need it. Good night."

He watched her walk away, wondering how much trouble this woman was going to be.

12

What did Carol think she was doing confronting Vincent like that? What did she hope to gain? Carol had to be honest and admit she did not know exactly what she was doing. All she knew was that she was shaking all over as she stood alone in the elevator. Confronting Vincent may not have been the prudent thing to do, but it was too late now. Amanda had told her that when she was speaking with Vincent on the phone, Amanda had heard a young woman's voice. How she knew it was a young woman, Carol could not guess. But when Carol was found in Tina's hospital room by Vincent, she felt cornered and decided to play out the cards she was holding. It was a bluff, but that was all she had.

From his behavior, Carol was certain Vincent was seeing someone while his wife was in a coma. If ever a man was trying to cover up a secret, it was Vincent.

But Carol would have to be careful, she knew. There was also something threatening in his manner. It was in his tone of voice and the way he looked at her. He had faced her squarely and did not shy away, unlike someone trying to cover up something. Vincent was full of pride and arrogance—she could see that now. Perhaps she had detected a trace of it in their brief encounters, but now she was sure of it.

What precisely she hoped to achieve by this she was not sure. All she knew was that she had the sword of Damocles hanging over her since Tina's fall, and it gave her a bit of relief to see someone else under the sword for a change.

But could this situation with Vincent be of any help to her at all? She was not certain. When and if Tina did come out of her coma, she might be blurry on what had occurred the day of her fall, so might not this thing with Vincent keep her mind occupied enough that she would not remember Carol's role in her accident? That seemed quite a stretch, not to mention insensitive. But Carol felt she was in a tight spot that she was exploring all types of strategies. Perhaps finding out more about this woman Vincent was seeing would be to her advantage.

It took Carol only a day to form a plan of action. After work, she stopped at home and loaded up a few things in a bag—a book, some protein bars, a bag of cookies, a few water bottles, and chewing gum. She brewed a large coffee and poured it in a travel mug. She drove to Tina's street and parked partway down the street, close enough where she could keep an eye on the house. It was still light, so to help pass the time she pulled out her novel and read. Amanda had given her this book. It was called *The Solicitor's Daughter*, and the story involves a young woman who falls in love with one of her father's clients.

Carol occasionally checked her watch. She remembered Det. Jarmon said that Vincent arrived home from work at about six o'clock.

Six o'clock came and went. An hour later Carol started to wonder if this was a good idea. Stakeouts never seemed this long and boring for detectives on police shows. Patience: that is what she needed. Relax. Relax. Breathe. Long deep breaths. That's better.

She was startled when someone violently knocked on the passenger-side window. Carol turned to see an angry-looking older man staring at her.

"What are you doing here?" he yelled. "Why are you parked outside my house? If you have no business here, get out! Get out of here before I call the police! Go on, git!"

She was so shaken at the man's sudden and aggressive appearance she fumbled out an apology but could not get the car started. The man continued to rant at her, and she was afraid he might come over to her side of the car and harass her further or even pull her out of the vehicle. She got the car started and drove away. Carol turned off the street but did not go very far. She had to pull over and calm down. Perhaps she should simply go home, she thought. If the police did show up, how would she explain her presence? It wouldn't be prudent to say that she suspected Vincent of putting Tina in the hospital. Vincent would turn around and accuse her. He had practically said so at the hospital. Best to keep a low profile with the police. Detective Jarmon may have acted disinterested, but the guy made her feel like a suspect. Jarmon's behavior may have only been an act to lull Carol into a false sense of security. She hoped never to see him again.

She sat behind the steering wheel thinking. This was

stupid. She looked at her watch. Vincent should have been home by now. Why wasn't he? He stopped off at the hospital, you fool, she berated herself. He most likely stopped off there every day to put in an appearance. Oh, what a good husband he is. He visits his poor wife every day. Isn't he thoughtful? What a load of crap!

He would get to the hospital at about six, he would stay an hour, and then he'd go to pick up his girlfriend. They go out to dinner—No. Vincent would not want to be seen out with another woman. They would pick up dinner and come back to Vincent's house. Carol suspected there was a good chance that she would be out late tonight.

She chose another spot on the street, away from the grumpy old man. She did not want to see him again. Soon after nine-thirty, a car came down the road. Carol ducked down in her seat. The car turned into the driveway of Tina and Vincent's house. The garage door went up automatically. The car drove into the attached garage, and the door closed automatically. In a minute, lights came on in the house. Through the window, a silhouette moved. No, two silhouettes.

Carol wished she hadn't drunk that large coffee. She had to pee so badly. Maybe she could knock on the door and ask Vincent if she could use the bathroom.

She desperately wanted to get a look at Vincent's friend. Carol got out of the car and very quietly closed the car door. She went up to the house and went around the side where it was dark. She could not wait any longer. Taking a quick look around, she dropped her pants and urinated near the house. Ahhh, that felt good. That done, she chose a window and gazed in. No movement. Going around the back she found another window and looked inside. She heard voices, but they were muffled. Vincent! Carol ducked down. Did he see her? Should she run now? It would be bad if she were caught spying on him. The muffled voices resumed. They sounded normal. Carol cautiously looked back through the window. There she was! She saw the woman. Carol could not see the woman's face clearly, but she could tell the woman was younger, maybe twenty-five, with blonde hair and a good figure. Turn around, honey, so I can get a good look at you. The woman turned. Carol could see her clearly, now. She knew this woman! But from where? So anxious and surprised at seeing the woman, Carol accidentally bumped her head against the window. There was a slight tap in the glass! Carol ducked down. She was certain they heard her. Carol kept low and ran in the direction of her car. She was only halfway there when she heard a door open. Despite it being dark, there were streetlights and Carol was sure to be seen. She was near a car parked on the street and she ducked behind it. Her heart raced and her breath came in quick gasps as she crouched and listened for any sound of pursuit. She waited. Nothing. She heard a door close, and Carol slowly raised her head. Nothing moved. There was no one on the street other than her. Standing up she casually made her way back to her car.

Once inside her car, Carol felt somewhat safer. She considered going home, then reconsidered. Maybe she was good at this spying thing. She decided to stay and keep watch. Hours later, Vincent's garage door went up and his car pulled out. Carol followed them.

She hung back a bit so as not to be detected, but even from there Carol could see that there were two people in the car. Vincent must be driving his girlfriend home, she thought. It may be advantageous to know where his cutey lived.

Just then she remembered when and where she had seen that woman in Vincent's house. It was in Vincent's house a year ago last Christmas. Tina was having an open house during the holiday season, and she was showing off the house. That young woman was from Vincent's office—junior assistant, or some such. Looks like Miss Junior Assistant got a promotion. What was her name? Victoria? Valerie? Violet? No, it wasn't Violet. She couldn't correctly recall.

The two cars headed north on the 101, then on to 114 to Pinardville. Lucky for Carol traffic was light, and she had no trouble following Vincent's car from a distance. In Pinardville, Vincent pulled up to an apartment building. He walked his assistant to the door, where he hesitated, looked around then kissed her goodnight. Wow! That is not a friendly kiss you give your assistant. She went into the building and Vincent walked back to his car, which he parked at the curb.

Carol had parked about half a block away. She watched Vincent standing by his car. He looked around, then looked down as if making a decision. He started walking down the street.

"Now where is he going?" Carol said out loud. He was walking on the street coming directly toward her car. "Oh, shit!" Her thoughts raced about what she should do. She could drive off like a coward, and he would surely see her, or she could hold her position. He had already seen her. No use fleeing. Carol decided to stay.

Vincent walked up quite casually and tapped lightly on Carol's window.

"Why are you following me?" he asked.

She lowered the window a bit. "I'm not following you."

"You were parked on my street and followed me from Bedford."

She did not respond. Her head turned in the direction of his assistant's apartment building. He looked at the building as well, then turned back to Carol.

"Why don't we go somewhere for a coffee?" he said in a friendly tone.

"It's pretty late for coffee."

"Order whatever you want. I'm buying. There is a nice coffee shop right down the street. Perhaps we should talk."

"Okay," she said. "I'll follow you."

They sat across from one another at a table in the coffee shop, their drinks in front of them. Vincent had an intense stare. Carol met his gaze.

"Why are you watching me, Carol?"

At least he remembered her name.

"I'm curious who you are sleeping with while your wife is in the hospital in a coma."

"You mean that woman I just dropped off? She is my assistant from work."

"Pretty affectionate for an assistant. Do you usually take your assistant home with you?"

"We've been working long hours at the office. I thought it would be a nice change to get out of the office and get some work done in a more personal setting."

"In your house—while your wife is away."

"Yes."

"Is that the best story you could come up with, Vincent?"

Vincent hung his head in thought. He wasn't proud of his behavior, but he no longer saw reason to deny it. She knew.

"I don't see how it is any of your business," he said.

"Tina is my friend, and I care about her. All the women in the group care about her."

"If you don't think I care deeply about Tina, you're wrong," he said. Vincent was able to speak calmly but kept a forceful tone. His dark features appeared even darker. Carol did not doubt that Vincent could be dangerous. It was this dangerous attribute that gave her an idea.

"You say you care about Tina, maybe you even love her," she said. "But if the authorities were to find out about... what is her name? Valerie?"

"Vanessa."

"Vincent and Vanessa—that's cute. Let's say, Det. Jarmon finds out about Vanessa, he might begin to suspect you had something to do with Tina's accident."

"What do you mean?" This caught him by surprise.

"Det. Jarmon might think that maybe you came home early that day. Tina found out about Vanessa, and the two of you got into a fight over your extramarital shenanigans."

"That's bullshit," he said, with the same calm control. Carol detected a trace of anger there.

"You look pretty fit, Vincent, pretty strong. You could overpower a woman like Tina. I bet you have quite a temper if you're provoked."

"Are you looking to find out?"

"You see, that's the kind of talk that makes you a prime suspect."

"If I was responsible for Tina's injury, I wouldn't try to make it look like an accident."

"You might if you panicked."

"I certainly would not have put those slippers on her feet to make it look like she slipped and fell."

"You might, if you wanted it to look like she slipped and fell."

He smiled slyly. "No, I wouldn't have put those slippers on her feet. You see, she hated those slippers. She made them, sure, but she didn't like them. Tina said that they were good enough for you and those other women, but she said she would not be caught dead in them."

"But she almost was."

"She didn't put those slippers on her feet. Someone else did. Someone who did not know that she hated them."

"Well, Vincent, we only have your word that Tina hated those slippers."

"Let us say that I am telling the truth," Vincent said with a conspiratorial tone. "If Tina did indeed hate those slippers, that means someone else put them on her feet. So, we must ask ourselves: who would have put them on her feet, and why?"

Carol shook her head.

"No idea?" he said. "Let us speculate: Tina argued with someone, they struggled, and she fell. That much you have already said yourself. There is poor Tina lying on the floor, her head cracked open and blood on the floor. The person does not call anyone, not an ambulance, and not the police. They panic. They need to make it look like an accident as if Tina slipped and fell. What does this person do? They put a pair of those knitted slippers on Tina's feet. Who could have done such a thing? Someone familiar with the slippers, that means one or more of the four women from your knitting group."

"Cross-stitch group."

"By your own admission, you were the last one to see my wife before she fell. Perhaps you even saw her after she fell."

"If your theory is correct, maybe one of the other women in the group came back after I left."

"That does not sound very plausible."

"Neither does it seem plausible that I had anything to do with it."

"It makes as much sense as blaming me. Why would I get in a struggle with Tina?"

"We already went over that, remember? —Vanessa."

Vincent considered this and had to privately admit that Carol had a good point. But he knew he had nothing to do with Tina's fall. Carol, on the other hand, was a reasonable candidate. He felt there was something about her, and her behavior.

"Why did you stay after the others left?" he asked.

"Because Tina asked me to stay to help clean up. Ask Amanda, she heard it all."

The two of them sat there in what could be considered a stalemate. It would do neither of them any good to pursue this line of blame and suspicion.

"What do we do now?" Carol asked.

"I suggest we go to neutral corners and stop trying to put the blame for Tina on each other. Also, we refrain from any future contact, and that means no parking outside my house, no following me around in your car, and no contact with Vanessa."

"I can live with that," Carol said, and like a gunfighter from an old western, she stood up slowly and backed out the door.

13

Carol thought it best to keep her contact with Vincent to herself. She would have loved to share it with the other women, but it may raise more questions about her own actions—questions she did not wish to answer.

She was not certain how she could use what she learned about Vincent and his dalliance, but it was good to know. What bothered her most was that Vincent seemed to suspect Carol of having a hand in Tina's accident. His thinking had been almost the exact scenario of what had happened. Only a devious person thinks like that.

The next cross-stitch meeting was scheduled at Harriet's house. Harriet lived in the same house for forty years. It was the house she and her husband bought when they found out she was pregnant with their first child, and they needed a bigger place. It became a household of five and it must have been a very active place—baseball practice, dance rehearsals, doctor's appointments, and the kid's friends coming over. The high school years saw everyone coming and going, the kids staying up late studying, dating, and getting into a bit of trouble now and then. College, empty nest, then Cliff passed away. Now Harriet was alone in a house too big for her, but she could not see herself moving out into a smaller place.

Harriet lived in an older neighborhood, away from the higher-end homes like Tina's. It was funny, Carol thought, Tina's house was twice as big for half as many people.

When Carol pulled up to the house, Harriet and Margaret were out front looking at the flower garden. She did not see Amanda's car. Carol wouldn't be the last one to arrive today.

She grabbed her craft case and walked over to the older women. Harriet greeted Carol warmly with a hug and a kiss on the cheek. Margaret gave Carol a nod and a bit of a smile. Margaret was not the warmest of people, Carol thought.

"How do you like the garden?" Harriet asked. "Margaret has been a great help. She really has a green thumb."

Margaret took the compliment in her usual fashion—unresponsive as if nothing was said.

Harriet could not help but show off her yellow roses, pink cosmos, purple foxglove, and violets, there were white daisies and lilies of the valley, orange chrysanthemums, and clematis growing on a weathered wooden trellis.

Harriet had been expounding on how she and Margaret moved the flowers around so the roses would get more sun and the astilbe would get more shade when Amanda pulled up.

When Amanda got out of her car, Carol pretended to look at her wristwatch and called out, "I was just going to call you to make sure you remembered."

Amanda raised her craft bag and said in a loud voice, "I feel the itch—the itch to stitch!"

They welcomed Amanda, and Carol had to listen and wait for Harriet to show Amanda the flower garden and give the exact same talk. It was obvious that Harriet was proud of her flowers, but not so proud that she did not give Margaret her due.

Inside they gathered in Harriet's living room which probably looked the same as it did twenty years ago. Everything appeared outdated. Harriet had one of her best cross-stitch projects framed and on the wall. In the center of the coffee table was a cut crystal vase with freshly cut flowers from her garden.

Each woman chose a chair and got out their cross-stitch. The chair Tina usually sat in remained vacant. No one mentioned that it felt strange for them to meet without Tina. It was certain that Tina was on everyone's mind.

"How is that new cross-stitch coming along, Carol?" Harriet asked.

Amanda came over to see the progress Carol had made.

"Why, that's your old cross-stitch," Amanda said. "Where is the other, the old-fashioned town?"

"Carol, aren't you working on that cross-stitch?" Harriet asked, sounding disappointed.

"It's a UFO," Carol said, which was an axiom for Unfinished Object. It referred to a cross-stitch project that someone got tired of or could not find the motivation to finish.

"It was beautiful," Harriet said. "I was looking forward to you finishing it. You could enter it in a competition."

"Yes, Carol, it was very good," Amanda added.

"Maybe I'll finish it one day, but for now I want to concentrate on this one," Carol said, with a hint of finality.

"It's just as well you leave the other and work on this one," Margaret said. Carol did not know what Margaret meant by that.

Everyone dropped the subject and the room fell silent, but not for very long.

"Has anyone called to see how Tina is doing?" Margaret asked.

Carol looked at the others and gave her shoulders a shrug.

"I called Vincent the other day," Amanda said. "He said there was no change."

"Did you ask if Tina opened her eyes again?" Harriet asked.

"No, but I think Vincent would have mentioned it. He said there was no change, so I have to assume she didn't open her eyes."

"Was Vincent with a young woman when you spoke with him this time?" Carol asked Amanda.

It was obvious to Carol from Amanda's expression that she had not shared this with Harriet and Margaret.

"What's this, now?" Harriet asked the two younger women. She appeared shocked. "What is this about Vincent and some woman?"

Carol turned to Amanda and shrugged, as if to say, You said it, now you own it.

Amanda almost looked reluctant to talk about it, which to Carol was strange since Amanda loved to gossip and liked to be the first one to know things. If knowledge was power, then Amanda craved the power of knowing something other people did not know. Carol, on the other hand, did not plan on sharing what she had discovered about Vincent and his assistant. She would have to explain why she staked out Vincent's house and then followed him in her car. Best to let this entire matter come from Amanda.

Amanda told Harriet and Margaret about calling Vincent and hearing a woman's voice on the telephone.

"And you think that means... what?" Margaret posed.

Amanda looked a bit shocked. "Isn't it obvious? Vincent is seeing some young floozy while his wife lies in a hospital in a coma!"

"That is a bit of a stretch, dear," Harriet said, shaking her head.

"You are assuming a lot," added Margaret.

Carol felt the urge to scream, *No! She's right! Vincent is having an affair! Amanda has it down, cold! I saw them together! I know where she lives! Her name is Vanessa!* But she simply sat there trying to look composed.

"What do you think, Carol?" Harriet asked.

Again, Carol shrugged, as if the matter did not overly concern her. "I don't know. There could be a reasonable explanation for Amanda hearing a woman's voice."

"Name one," Amanda asked, with a hint of skepticism.

Carol paused in thought. "She might have been Vincent's assistant from work, and they needed to get out of the office and work in a more relaxed setting."

"That is so lame, Carol," Amanda countered. "That sounds like the lame excuse Vincent would come up with if he were caught. I heard the woman ask if they were going out."

"They probably hadn't had dinner and were trying to decide whether to order in or dine out."

"Carol, why are you defending this guy?" Amanda asked.

"I'm not. I just don't see jumping to conclusions."

"Perhaps Carol is right," Harriet said. "Maybe it's best not to make any hasty judgments."

"You'll see I'm right," Amanda said with ire. "Vincent is

carrying on behind Tina's back. It's despicable. You mark my words."

"Consider them marked," said Carol.

"I hope it's not true," Margaret said. "I cannot stand someone breaking their vows."

"How is that?" Carol said, confused.

Margaret turned to her. "Tina and Vincent were married in a church. They took a vow, an oath to love one another, forsaking all others. If Vincent is indeed seeing someone else, that means he's broken his oath. I dislike it when someone breaks their oath."

Carol somehow felt that Margaret was speaking of her. "I'm getting divorced, Margaret. Am I an oath-breaker as well? Do you dislike me because I broke an oath, because I broke my vows?"

Margaret did not respond. She looked at Carol with her usual grim countenance. Harriet decided to intervene.

"All right, ladies. No one is judging anyone—not anyone in this group and not Vincent. I, for one, do not want Tina's unfortunate circumstances to drive us apart. Tina would not want this either. I suggest no more talk of Vincent."

The four of them appeared to agree to this and they all sat in silence for a long while. Just after 2:30, Harriet brought out light snacks and drinks. She did not serve alcohol, so Carol had to settle for a soft drink, and later a cup of tea.

They were all standing around Harriet's kitchen table where she had laid out their drinks and snacks. Margaret approached Carol.

"I did not mean any offense when I spoke about oaths, Carol," she said, with as much humility as Margaret could muster. It may not have been humble, but it was sincere.

"I know Margaret. No offense taken."

They did not hug, but Margaret nodded approvingly.

Margaret went to turn away but reconsidered. "Why did you stop working on that other cross-stitch?" Margaret asked bluntly. The question caught Carol by surprise.

"Oh... you know... it was... difficult."

Margaret nodded again. "I think it was good that you stopped. I rather like those flowers in a vase." Then she turned and ambled off.

Carol was tempted to ask Margaret what she meant by that, but she thought it best to let it go.

After a sufficient break, the group resumed their cross-stitching.

Margaret was still working on her kitchen and baked pies, Harriet had switched from the beautiful angel to work on a single pink rose stretched in a wooden hoop, and Amanda was close to finishing her cat.

For Carol, this meeting was very different from the last one, and it wasn't just the absence of Tina and her condition. During the last meeting when she was working on Smith Falls, everyone was impressed with Carol's work. The women were asking her opinion and were holding her in high regard. Now Carol felt she had dropped down a peg or two, and it did not feel good. Carol told herself she had to sacrifice her status in the group for the sake of the cross-stitch. It was because of the cross-stitch she discovered Smith Falls. For now, she had to go by the rules set out in the cross-stitch, and not let anyone see it. She knew she would complete it one day and it would surely win first prize at the Spring Fair, but for now, the cross-stitch must keep a low profile.

"Did Det. Jarmon ask anyone about the piece of cross-stitch chart they found in Tina's hand?" Amanda asked, rather innocently.

Carol froze and the room went silent again. Be calm, she told herself. Calm, calm, calm.

"What was that, Amanda?" Harriet asked.

"When Det. Jarmon questioned me about the day Tina had her fall, he showed me a piece of the chart they found in Tina's hand. He asked me what it was, if it looked familiar, and if it were mine. Did he ask anyone else?"

The other three looked at one another rather uncomfortably. They each slowly nodded.

"Yes, he showed it to me," Harriet said.

"Yes, I saw it," Margaret said. "He showed it to me."

Carol nodded. "He told me about it." Everyone looked at Carol as if there should be more. "He asked if he could see my chart. I guess he might have thought the torn piece could be mine."

Still, they continued to look at Carol.

"Did you show him your chart?" Harriet asked.

"Yes, I showed it to him. There was no rip in my chart."

"Why do you think Tina had a torn piece of chart in her hand?" Margaret asked.

"Do you think it might be some kind of clue?" Harriet asked them all.

They all thought about this.

"Do you think it might have something to do with Vincent?" Amanda said.

"How?" Carol asked, incredulously. "I think you're fixated on Vincent."

"I am not!" Amanda said petulantly.

"Amanda, how do you think Vincent may be connected with a piece of chart?" Harriet asked calmly.

Amanda thought for a moment. It became clear that she hadn't given it much thought and had just blurted it out.

"Maybe," she said slowly as if she was still grasping for an explanation. "Maybe Vincent put a piece of the torn chart in Tina's hand to draw interest away from him."

"Did Det. Jarmon tell anyone else that Tina was found with a pair of those knitted slippers on her feet?" Harriet asked.

The room went silent again for a moment.

"Yes, Jarmon told me that as well," Margaret said.

"He told me," Amanda said.

Carol nodded. "Yes, he mentioned it to me as well."

"Does anyone else find it strange that Tina was not wearing those slippers during the meeting, but she was found with them on her feet?" Harriet asked.

"It was a little strange," Margaret said.

"Now that you mention it," said Amanda, "it was peculiar that Tina was wearing them when she was found."

"You know, I slipped and almost fell in those slippers," Carol said.

"Yes, I know, so did I," Harriet said.

"It is no wonder that she fell in those things," Carol said.

"But did she?" Margaret asked.

"What do you mean, dear?" Harriet asked, but it was Amanda who spoke up.

"Maybe someone put them on Tina to make it look like a slip and fall."

"Who would do that?" Harriet wanted to know.

"I think I know!" Amanda said.

"Let me guess," Carol said. "It was Vincent."

"Well, why not?" said Amanda. "If Vincent was responsible for Tina's "accident"—she used air quotes when she said accident— "then, maybe he put slippers on her feet to make out as if she slipped and fell."

"That is just devious," Margaret said.

"It is just so hard to believe Vincent would do that," Harriet said. "It's hard to believe anyone would do such a despicable thing. Carol, what do you think?"

Carol's head swam. It was important for her to stay calm and lucid.

"I think that after we left, Tina kicked off her heels and put on a pair of slippers. Maybe she wanted to see if they were slippery. I think Tina picked up a torn piece of a chart from the floor or a chair—you know how neat she was—and she still was holding it when she slipped and fell. It was a terrible accident, but that is what I think."

The other women stopped to consider this. It all sounded reasonable, and they nodded their heads in acceptance. This pretty much brought an end to any conspiracy theories within the group. It was too bad, for they were secretly enjoying talking about these things, and it was like Carol had put a damper on their fun.

When it was time to go, Harriet told all the ladies to take a flower from the crystal vase on the table. When each woman chose the flower they wanted, Harriet, like Ophelia from Hamlet, would say what each flower represented.

Margaret went first and chose a violet.

"Violet for faith, mystical awareness, inspiration, and spiritual passion. How appropriate."

Amanda went next and could not seem to make up her mind. Finally, she chose a white lily of the valley.

"Lily of the valley for sweetness and purity. That's you, dear."

Carol chose a yellow rose.

"A rose for love, passion, and admiration," Harriet said, and then leaned forward and, as she had done to the other women, kissed Carol on the cheek.

14

When Carol arrived home, she put her rose in a water-filled mason jar and set it on her kitchen table. She made herself a drink and went into her craft room. She had recently bought a floor stand for her frame holder so she would not have to hold the frame while working on Smith Falls. The work was coming along very well, she thought, as she stood looking down at it. It was difficult not to take it with her to the monthly meeting. She wished only to work on this cross-stitch and show it off. The work garnered her praise and admiration from her friends, and it would surely take first prize at the next craft fair. But Carol knew that keeping it private for now was more important than all those things. She did not want to break any of the rules again.

Carol felt drawn to the cross-stitch. When she wasn't working on it, she was content to simply look at it and study all the aspects of it. She knew every stitch. She felt an affinity between her and her cross-stitch. It is always so when someone creates something. Your creation is a part of you—part of who and what you are and is a reflection of you. Smith Falls was never far from her mind.

Still, Carol knew her cross-stitch was simply more than a craft or a hobby. This was a doorway to another time and place—Smith Falls. Carol knew Smith Falls was real. It was not a mere dream or her imagination. She had been there, interacted with its residents, and experienced the place. Was Smith Falls her destiny, she wondered. She wanted to go back, that was certain, but did she wish to live there permanently? Could she? At times she thought Smith Falls was too good to be true. Could any world be that idyllic? Were there some aspects of Smith Falls that were being kept from her? And if so, what were they and why were they being kept from her? If she went to Smith Falls again, might she never be able to return? Might she forever be trapped in that world?

Would that be so bad, she wondered. Was Smith Falls any worse than the life she was living now? Every day she lived under the threat that Tina would come out of her coma and relate what had happened. Every day Carol could be found out, then everyone would know what type of person she was. And what if Tina were to die from her injuries? Would Carol be responsible for her death?

Yes, she would.

Carol had struggled with Tina in Tina's house. Tina fell and hit her head and Carol just left her lying and bleeding on the floor. Not only that, but she even put those slippers on her feet to make it appear as if Tina slipped on the tile floor. Did all that add up to her being a bad person?

Yes, it did.

She should be punished for that alone, and that is not counting all her other sins. Sins, she thought. Carol had not thought in the context of sins since she was a little girl. Sins were bad and sinful acts were punishable. Should she be punished for her sins?

Yes, she should.

But it wasn't her fault, what happened to Tina—not entirely. If Tina hadn't taken her chart, this would not have even happened. Maybe the cross-stitch was as much to blame. No—the cross-stitch is not evil, it is beautiful. Smith Falls was her escape, her refuge from all her troubles.

Was it a coincidence that she found Malum Crafts, and that woman gave her the cross-stitch? It was such a bizarre experience. Then, there was that creepy guy she saw that time she went back. He was the reason she had not returned to the craft store again, but she needed to go back now, she felt. Carol needed some answers. Would they think she was crazy if Carol told them she had been to Smith Falls? No, they would understand. They would understand perfectly. She had to go back to the craft store.

Someone knocking on Carol's front door brought her out of her musings. She closed the door to her craft room and locked it. Peering out the window she saw Gary's car. Damn! She totally forgot Gary was coming today.

Opening the door, she greeted him coolly.

"I thought you said you would call first," she said, trying to look a little put-out.

"I did," he said. "You didn't answer, and I came anyway. Where is your phone?"

"It's around," she said in a manner that said it was none of his business—which it wasn't.

Garry stood there. "Are you going to invite me in?"

"Come in."

Gary stepped in gingerly as if he were afraid to disturb anything. He remembered how he and Carol had found this house and how excited they both were. The house was big enough even if they had two kids. With three, they would have to move to a bigger place. But that was not to be. Now they had to sell the house.

"We have to sell the house, Carol," he said. "I've already spoken with a few real estate agents. We'll have to pick one and they will get a sign on the lawn. Carol, do you understand?"

She had been listening to him with a blank expression as if he had been speaking in a foreign language.

"Yes, I understand. No, wait, is there any way I can keep the house? There must be some way."

"You can't afford the payments."

"I suppose a reconciliation is out of the question."

"We are way past reconciliation, Carol."

"Why?"

"Why?" he repeated. "You wanted this, remember? Remember what you said? That you didn't want to be married anymore. I want to be independent. You remember that?"

"Where am I supposed to live?"

"You'll have some money from the settlement."

"Yeah, I got the papers from the lawyer. How am I supposed to live on that?"

"This is what you wanted—independence! Remember?"

"This is Monica's idea, isn't it?" Carol said petulantly. "She put you up to this, didn't she?"

"Don't bring Monica into this, Carol. She has nothing to do with this. This was your doing. I suppose I should have fought harder for our marriage, but I didn't."

They both went quiet for several minutes.

"Maybe you could find a smaller place and get a roommate," he proposed.

She had practically no close friends except for the women in her cross-stitch group. Her family was out of state, and she was not exactly on good terms with them. It seemed she had burned too many bridges in her life.

"Once we settle on an agent, they will call you to schedule an open house," Gary said.

"Open house?"

"Yeah. People will want to see the house before they buy it."

"I guess they would."

"How much do you think the house is worth?" she asked.

"After you subtract the house agent's commission, not to

mention that the house is not paid off, it won't be as much as you might think."

Carol nodded absent-mindedly. She was thinking about the future open houses. She would not be able to keep the cross-stitch out but would have to be hidden away every time someone wanted to see the house.

"I'll call you and give you a heads-up on when to expect someone to show up," Gary said. "In the meantime, if it's okay with you, I'll come over and mow the lawn and clean up the yard some. If you could clean up the inside, make everything neat and… presentable, it will make it easier to sell the place and get a decent price."

Carol nodded again. She could not help feeling that her life was crashing down upon her head. She saw him out and could not remember if she even said goodbye. In the kitchen, she poured herself a drink. Taking it into the backroom Carol studied her cross-stitch. She wished she were in Smith Falls right now, away from all this mess of a life. Maybe if she worked on it until she fell asleep, she would find herself there, on a sunny day with her friends. She could go for a walk with Mr. Walter Pennington, and he would recite poetry to her, and they would look longingly into each other's eyes.

But before all that happened, Carol needed some answers about the cross-stitch and Smith Falls, and she was determined to get them.

15

Carol got in her car and drove south on the 101. She was certain of easily finding Malum Crafts, but every time she thought she was on the right road, and it was just ahead, Carol found she was wrong. Sometimes it felt as if she were driving in circles. How could this be? She may not have a great sense of direction, but this was ridiculous. It almost felt like the first night she was searching for it.

The sun was setting in the west and her car was low on gas. She managed to find a gas station, the kind with two pumps, and an attendant who pumps the gas for you. The attendant was a thin middle-aged man who probably owned the place. He had a small garage with an old-style lift and a small store that sold sundries. When Carol paid for her gas, she asked the attendant if he knew Malum Crafts and how to get there. The man looked up and down the road. He asked her to repeat the name of the place. She did. Carol felt a chill run through her when the man shook his head and said he never heard of it.

Carol continued to search and the longer she drove, the more panic seemed to take over. A light film of perspiration broke out over her entire body, and her mouth went dry. It would be dark soon. This road looked familiar. If she did not find it on this road, she would go home.

"Son-of-a—" she said as the store appeared ahead of her. "Thank God!" she uttered and pulled up to the door. It was getting dark. She got out of the car and looked around for the crazy gravedigger. He was nowhere to be seen. Carol stood on the low wooden porch and the light above her head flickered and came on.

She opened the door, and the bell rang over her head. The place appeared empty. She remembered that smell. As she stepped gingerly into the store, the floorboards creaked. The only other sound was her own breathing. No one stood behind the counter. Carol peered over it to make sure.

"Hello?" Carol's voice cracked and sounded weak. No call came back.

She slowly walked the aisles looking at the extensive range of items. There were limitless colors of paints and paintbrushes, pallets, easels, and entire painting kits. There were markers, crayons, colored pencils, coloring kits, and sketchbooks. There were kits to make jewelry, mandala coasters, scrapbooks, shadow boxes, paint-by-numbers, and foam clay. There were wood-burning kits, dollhouse kits, glues, and pastes. There were tools and accessories for all types of needlework; crocheting, knitting, needlepoint, embroidery, and quilting.

Carol walked on until she came to the framed cross-stitch work high on the walls she had seen when last she was here. She looked up at them and marveled at the workmanship and beauty. She knew Smith Falls would rival these when she was done.

Carol sensed another presence very close. She turned and started at the appearance of the woman whom she took to be the owner standing right beside her. Carol had not heard the woman's approach.

"You startled me," Carol said. The woman said nothing. "Do you remember me? I was in here before." The woman nodded. "My name is Carol Crane. I'm sorry, I forgot your name."

The woman stood there with a deadpan expression, sleepy-eyed, and flat-mouthed. "Agatha," she finally said. Her voice was as dull as her expression.

"Agatha," Carol repeated. "Agatha... Malum?"

Agatha neither confirmed nor denied this.

Carol cleared her throat. "Agatha, I have a few questions about my cross-stitch. Do you remember the cross-stitch you sold me?"

"Sold you? Do you have a receipt?"

"Ah, no. I guess I meant to say the cross-stitch you gave me. Do you remember the kit? Smith Falls?"

Agatha nodded slowly.

"I just thought I'd ask, uhm, do you think... is there something... special... or out of the ordinary... about the... cross-stitch?"

"What do you think?"

"Oh... I think... it's... uhm... extraordinary. It's quite... lovely. The way the floss brings the entire image... alive. It possesses a 3D effect. You almost expect the people to walk right off the cross-stitch. Has that ever happened? Has a character ever done that?"

Agatha continued to stare mutely at her, and Carol could not tell if Agatha thought she was a bit crazy.

"You've been there, haven't you?" asked Agatha.

"Been where? Oh, you mean... Smith Falls? Uhm... yes, I've been there." Carol attempted to sound very casual about her visit to Smith Falls, but even as she admitted it, Carol felt uncomfortable talking about it.

"Let me ask you, Agatha; how is it possible? I mean... how?"

"It is a very special cross-stitch."

Carol felt somewhat deflated, as she was expecting more than that.

"Yes, the cross-stitch certainly is special," Carol said. "But why is it special?"

Agatha thought about this. "Any unique qualities it possesses are first from the materials; the linen, the thread, and the needle. Second, are the stitches, each coming in contact with those three materials. The stitches interlace with the linen and each stitch touches the other, creating an endless, seamless pattern. The pattern on the chart is remarkable in itself, as it reflects something... enchanted."

"Enchanted," Carol repeated.

Agatha continued. "Lastly comes the stitcher, the creator of the cross-stitch. That person becomes tied to the work—tied beyond any untying. All are connected like the stitches themselves—interlaced. Do you understand?"

Carol nodded that she did, but really, she did not understand. What Agatha was saying sounded beyond natural science—things that dwelt with the physical world—not to mention time and space. Agatha's statements were abstract, with no basis in reality. How was Carol to make sense of this?

"But how is it possible?" Carol persisted, wanting to know, and hoping to understand. "How does it work? How do I go there and how do I come back? It is real, isn't it? I mean, Smith Falls is real. It's a real place with real people."

"What do you think?"

"Please, don't," Carol said with a degree of irritability. "Please, don't give me any psychiatrist crap. I need to know. Is it all real?"

Agatha appeared neither flustered nor offended at Carol's attitude. Indeed, nothing seemed to disturb her. She was the epitome of dead calm. Her mien was devoid of emotion. She was practically robotic.

"There are worlds that exist within worlds, outside of worlds, between worlds," Agatha said, and her voice was so monotone, lacking any intonation or inflection, that Carol was almost hypnotized by her words. It was like listening to strange alien concepts.

"If we, who live in the present, can visualize a past and future, why not other worlds? The world of the dead, the world of the unborn. Worlds of mists and shadows where nothing is clear, and no one is who they appear to be. Ghost worlds, and lands of gods and demons. There are countless worlds, some beyond our grasp, but not all. Some worlds can be breached, and Smith Falls is only one of many. You have been given a great gift, Carol. You can pass over to another world, another life. Isn't that what you wanted—another life?"

Carol thought of the last part. She secretly wanted another life. A chance to start again. Her life here was falling apart and going nowhere. Smith Falls was her chance for another life, a better life. It was indeed a dream world.

"But what about Tina?" Carol asked. "Do you know about Tina? Do you know what happened to Tina?"

Agatha nodded. "Do you know why it happened?"

Carol shook her head. "No."

Agatha's face held a hint of doubt. "I think you do."

"No, I don't," Carol said, more forcefully.

"You broke the rules," Agatha said. "You showed the cross-stitch to your friends. It was a very dangerous thing to do. You let someone else take the chart. You lost a piece of it. That all adds up to disaster."

"How do you know all that? I need you to tell me how you know all that!"

"It is enough that you know that I know."

Carol thought of all that Agatha had said. She felt like crying, but what good would that do? She'll cry when she gets home. Would she get home, she wondered.

"What do I do now?" she asked Agatha. "Will I be able to finish the cross-stitch?"

"You must finish it."

"What do you mean, I must finish it? What if I don't? What if I've had enough? What if I just want to wash my hands of the whole thing?"

Carol was very close to crying now. She may not make it until she gets home.

Agatha said, "Every time you deviate from the rules... let me just say that every time you deviate from the rules it will be bad."

"Bad?" Carol repeated. "What do you mean by bad? Describe bad."

"Harmful, dangerous, unpleasant, unwelcomed—does that explain it?"

"Why didn't you tell me all this before you gave it to me?" Carol raised her voice. "There is no way I would have started the thing if I knew all this! You tricked me!"

"You wanted it," Agatha said. "You wanted a blue ribbon. You wanted to prove you were good at something."

"It's not worth it!"

"You don't know that."

Carol wondered what she meant by that.

"Listen, Agatha, can't I just give you back the cross-stitch? Can't you simply take it back? Take it off my hands?"

"It does not work that way. You started something that you must finish."

"This is ridiculous! It's not right! It's not fair!" Carol had grown very upset. Her face grew taught and her voice angry. Agatha remained unchanged.

Carol passed her hand nervously across her forehead and

took a minute to compose herself.

"Will Tina come out of her coma?" Carol asked. "Will she live?"

Agatha gave a slight shrug.

"That, you don't know," Carol said, frustrated.

"Much depends on you."

"Great," Carol said, with a combination of sarcasm and doom.

"Much of this is academic," Agatha said. "You want to finish the cross-stitch. There exists a need inside of you to finish it."

"You know that? How is it you know that?"

"It is more important that you know it."

Carol nodded. A lone tear ran down her face. She wiped it with the heel of her hand.

"Will I be able to return to Smith Falls?" she asked.

"Again, much depends on you."

"What happens when I finish the cross-stitch?"

"I do not know who can answer that question."

Carol's shoulders grew incredibly heavy. With her head hung low she made her way to the door. Opening it the bell rang and she stepped out into the night. The light over the porch flickered and went out. There was enough light for her to find her car. She got in and drove.

16

Carol never had half as much trouble finding her way home compared to finding Malum Crafts. She felt foolish that she did not use the GPS on her phone so she could find her way back to Malum's if she needed to, but she could not find her phone. She must have left it at home. By the time she got home, Carol felt exhausted—physically and mentally. Everything Agatha had told her shook her to her core and clawed at her emotions. How could all this be happening?

How could she allow this to take over her life?

Time to be honest with herself; she had never taken an active or determinate role in her own life. She had gone through life without discernible effort or having any fine focus or purpose. She had been lazy. That is why she did not finish college, that is why she let her marriage degenerate. That is why she liked Smith Falls—it was a lazy existence. Carol did not like hard work or the idea of personal sacrifice. She lacked commitment, even with those things that mattered most.

Her phone rang. It was Harriet.

"Hello, Harriet."

"Hello Carol, how are you?" Carol detected a bit of urgency in her voice. "I've been calling you and you didn't pick up. I was getting worried. I was considering driving over there, but I don't like driving at night. Are you certain you're all right?"

"Oh, sure, Harriet, I'm fine."

"Why didn't you pick up earlier?"

"I was out and forgot my phone at home."

"Oh, where did you go?"

"Just driving around. There is so much going on, that I felt I needed to get out and drive and get some fresh air."

"Do you mean Tina?"

"Yes, of course, Tina, but... Gary was over this afternoon, and we need to sell the house, I'm going to have to move and find a place to live."

"Do you have any ideas?"

"Not very many, I'm afraid."

"Oh, honey, I'm sorry you're going through this."

"Thank you."

"Where did you drive?"

"Pardon me?"

"When you were out, driving around—where did you go?"

"Uhm... you know... just around."

"Carol, the reason I wanted to speak with you was what

took place between you and Margaret."

"Margaret and me?"

"Yes, do you remember when you got a bit testy when Margaret brought up about people who break their vows?"

"Ooooh yes," Carol said. To be truthful she had forgotten all about it.

"I just wanted to assure you that Margaret meant no offense."

"No?"

"No."

"I don't see any other way to take it, Harriet. She made some derogatory reference to oath breakers. It is obvious that Margaret doesn't approve of married people getting a divorce."

"It's not that, Carol."

"You mean Margaret doesn't care if people get divorced?"

"No. I mean yes; I suppose she does. But when she said that she could not stand to see people break their vows... she was referring to herself."

"Herself? She was never married, was she?"

"Not in the manner you think."

"What are you saying?"

"Carol, what I am about to tell you is in strict confidence—do you understand?"

"I suppose so."

"There is no supposing about it. What I am about to tell you, you can never tell anyone. Do you promise?"

"Yes, I promise."

Harriet paused, and the line went quiet. Carol waited.

"Margaret used to be a Catholic nun," Harriet said. "She was a nun for years. Margaret took her final vows and received a ring, noting she was a bride of Christ. This vow is supposed to be until death, but Margaret left her order. It was not an easy decision for her, and she is not proud of what she did."

"Why did Margaret leave?"

"Carol, you don't need to know that part," Harriet said. "I

cannot tell you that. It would be up to Margaret if she wants you to know. I am breaking a confidence telling you this much."

"Don't worry, Harriet, I won't tell anyone, not even Margaret."

"What I want you to understand, is that if Margaret does get upset over the idea of breaking an oath, or a vow, she is agonizing over her own decision."

"I understand, Harriet."

"I hope so. Margaret and I have been friends for years. I knew her when she was a nun. I'll tell you something else about Margaret; I never met anyone, man or woman or child, who was so sensitive to bad people."

"What?"

"Margaret seems to have a sixth sense in detecting evil in people."

"How do you mean?"

Again, the line went quiet.

"It is a bit difficult to explain," Harriet said, hesitantly. "She has sometimes pointed out certain people to me who turned out to be bad people. A number of years ago a man contacted me about selling my house. He promised to get me more than the market value. He had a good reputation in southern New Hampshire. Luckily, on one of his visits to my house, Margaret happened to be there. When she met him, Margaret had an extraordinary look on her face. She pulled me aside immediately and told me not to do any business with the man. Margaret was so forceful I could not ignore her. To make a long story short, I did not do any business with that man, and months later he was facing fraud charges. People were scammed, many people lost their homes, and some lost sizeable deposits.

"There is one other instance that I will tell you. Do you remember that case in Portsmouth where the wife went missing, and there was a statewide alert, but she could not be found? The woman's husband went on the television to make a plea for the safe return of his wife. It was quite heartfelt and emotional, as I recall. Afterward, Margaret called me and told me that she had watched it on TV and after seeing the husband, Margaret believed he killed his wife. That is exactly what the police discovered four months later. He had taken her dead body across the state line into Maine. They found her body in Sebago Lake."

"Wow," was all Carol could say. She had a vague recollection of the case as it occurred years ago.

After a few more exchanges, Carol said goodbye to Harriet and hung up.

Carol was shaken. She always suspected Margaret had a secret history, but she had not considered anything like this. Did Margaret somehow know that she—Carol— was responsible for what happened to Tina? Did Margaret suspect that she was evil? Surely Margaret would have told Harriet if she did. Maybe Margaret did tell Harriet and that was why Harriet called tonight. Now you are getting paranoid, Carol thought to herself. Take a step back. Breathe deep.

Carol started to recall her interactions with Margaret since working on the Smith Falls cross-stitch. That first day at Tina's when everyone saw it, Margaret's reaction was a bit different. Amanda, Harriet, and even Tina thought the new cross-stitch Carol brought was exceptional, but Margaret's reaction was not as complimentary. What did Margaret say when she saw it? "Huh," was all she said. The day Carol went to the copy shop in Manchester and ran into Harriet and Margaret, they had lunch together. Margaret questioned Carol very suspiciously as if she knew what Carol was up to. At their last cross-stitch meeting when Carol told everyone she decided to stop working on Smith Falls and went back to Flowers in a Vase, Harriet and Amanda were disappointed, but Margaret said it was for the best.

Carol wondered what Margaret knew or suspected about the Smith Falls cross-stitch. Even more important; did Margaret have any inkling about Carol's involvement in Tina's accident?

One thing was certain; Carol would have to be extra careful when she found herself around Margaret.

17

Carol felt a perceptible difference in Smith Falls this time. The sun shone but there was no feeling of warmth. The air held no freshness. Indeed, the air tasted stale and bitter on her tongue. The usual noises—birds chirping, children laughing, horse-drawn carriages—all sounded muffled, or like a bad recording. Nothing appeared to have the clarity that had marked the town on her previous visits. There was a dullness that could not be described or pinpointed.

Chairs had been set up before the bandstand. People were seated or standing waiting for the outdoor concert to begin. A uniformed brass band dressed in black pants, red band jackets, and matching caps, sat on the bandstand awaiting the conductor. There were sounds of notes being played and last-minute preparations. They were waiting for the band leader.

Carol sat in one of the chairs in the middle of the audience. She turned to her left. There was Penelope Hope on her immediate left and next to her was Robert Crawford. They turned and smiled at Carol. There was something in those smiles that unnerved Carol. The smiles held no joy, no affection. They were fake smiles—smiles that hid some secret malevolence. It was like watching a pair of snakes smiling.

Carol turned slowly to her right. Mr. Walter Pennington sat next to her. He did not smile, instead, he wore an uncharacteristic scowl. Carol barely recognized him. What was going on? Was Smith Falls deteriorating—falling into corruption before her eyes? Had something terrible happened to the cross-stitch that was causing this? She had a very bad feeling that something was horribly wrong.

"Here comes the band leader," Penelope said, but Carol detected a change in her voice as if she were listening to a bad audio speaker.

All the heads of the attendees turned in the direction of the bandleader who was approaching the bandstand. Carol gasped when she saw the bandleader, for she swore it was Harriet Wolters. What was Harriet doing here? Was she able to cross over to Smith Falls? How? Carol's heart raced and her breath came quickly.

Harriet approached the bandstand, climbed the three steps to the raised platform, and took her place before the band with her back to the audience. She raised her hands and there was absolute silence for a few seconds, then the band broke out into a cacophony of music. Horns, drums, and cymbals clashed. Carol looked over the band and was surprised to see the tuba player was Amanda. She was blowing earnestly and with great effort into the tuba, but no sound came out. The band played on unceasingly. Everyone in the band sounded offkey. Her head began to hurt, and Carol wished they would stop playing. Then another set of figures caught Carol's attention. Approaching from down the street came two women. One was Margaret, with her usual dour expression and dressed in a nun's habit. She was pulling along Tina who wore a hospital gown with a white bandage around her head and a tube hung from her nose. Tina's steps were unsteady, and she walked like a zombie. They approached Carol and while the band played on Margaret pointed an accusing finger at Carol and then gestured to Tina. Carol could not hear Margaret's accusations as they were drowned out by the band's music, which grew louder and louder. Everyone around looked at Carol and their expressions turned hostile. Angry, distorted faces hemmed her in and drew closer. Carol knew Margaret was accusing her of hurting Tina and putting her in this condition. Carol tried to cry out, No! No! But no one could hear her over the music. Carol stood up and tried to run away but Penelope and Walter grabbed each of her arms and wouldn't let go of her. Carol kept screaming.

Carol woke up screaming. She was sitting up in her own bed, shocked and bewildered. Her chest felt like it would explode. A dream. Only a dream, her mind told her. Dream, hell! It was a nightmare! Gasping for air she clutched her chest as if trying to keep her heart from bursting out. Is this what a heart attack feels like, she wondered. Falling back down on her pillow, she lay there unmoving for several minutes, until that awful feeling subsided, and she had the strength and will to get out of bed.

Coffee, coffee, coffee. How she wished someone was there to make her a coffee. With trembling hands, she took a cup from the cupboard, put a pod in the machine, and pressed the button. Carol shuddered at the memory of the nightmare. Reality soon seeped in. Time to get ready to go to work.

After the morning shift at The Golden Griddle, Carol went to Crafty Business.

Irene was happy to see Carol and asked if she was keeping up with whatever cross-stitch project Carol was working on.

"You're in a cross-stitch group, aren't you?" Irene asked.

"Uhm, yes," Carol said, rather hesitantly.

"Good group of women?"

"Yes, they are. It's just that…"

"What is it?" Irene asked.

"I never told you, but one of the women in the group had a terrible accident at home. She slipped and fell and hit her head. She's in the hospital in a coma."

"Oh, dear!" Irene said, shocked. "That is awful!"

"Yes, it is. We're all very concerned."

"Is she married? How is her husband taking it?"

"Well… you know… he's coping the best he can. He sees her every day. She's in intensive care."

"That is simply dreadful. He must be devastated. You all must be."

"The entire matter is… so… difficult to deal with," Carol said.

"Thank you for telling me," Irene said, sincerely. "I'll pray for your friend and her family. Does she have children?"

"No. No children."

Carol felt better sharing the news about Tina with Irene. Irene really was a very nice woman. It also helped Carol keep her mind off of the nightmare she had. Her talk with Agatha and her conversation with Harriet must have all come together in her subconscious and conjured up that horrible dream. Of course, she could not deny that guilt, indelibly pressed upon her mind also had something to do with it.

A few hours later she had just about forgotten about the dream when a customer came into the shop. It was not the usual kind of customer. It was a man—and he was by himself. Now, of course, Carol had seen men come in the store, but almost every one of them was in tow behind their wife or girlfriend and they all had that look as if they did not want to be there. Most of the men who came in had that hangdog expression and their hands were thrust in their pockets, so they were not accidentally contaminated by anything.

Carol gasped when she recognized the customer. "Oh, my God!" she almost said aloud, trying not to show her shock and surprise. It was Det. Jarmon! She looked to the back of the store and was about to walk quickly to the back room, when Irene said, "Carol, could you see what this guy wants?"

Carol stammered out something and approached Jarmon.

He had been perusing the merchandise but looked up at Carol's approach.

"Can I help you find something?" she said.

"Oh, hi," he said with a surprised smile. He looked over her shoulder, then met her gaze. "Carol Crane. This is a coincidence. Do you work here?"

"Yes, I do. It is nice to see you again. Are you on duty?"

"No. It's my day off. This is my off-duty outfit," he said, touching his tie and thumbing the lapels of his jacket.

"It looks a lot like your on-duty outfit," she said.

He laughed. "That's good."

"Are you looking for something?"

"Yes, I am," he said, casting his gaze around the store, then back to her face. "I am looking for something for my mother. I was looking for something to keep her occupied, keep her hands moving and her mind active. I remembered talking to you and the members of your group and I thought maybe I would get my mother into cross-stitch or something."

"Is your mother crafty?"

"Oh, she's sly like a fox."

"No, I meant—"

"I know what you meant."

"Has she ever done any crafts—rug hooking, crocheting, or knitting?"

"I honestly don't know. She might have at one time."

"Cross-stitch is something anyone can do. We could start her off with a beginner's kit."

"A kit?"

"Yes, a kit has everything in it that a cross-stitcher needs—the needle, floss, chart, and Aida cloth. A kit keeps you from having to buy all that individually. How does that sound?"

"Sounds... like I'm buying a kit," he said, smiling.

Carol showed him some kits that were in the store.

"Have you worked here for a long time?" Jarmon asked.

"Six, maybe seven years, I guess."

"Do you like it?"

"Sure. It's a job—as good as another."

Between the two of them, they chose a kit and Carol was ringing him up at the register. "I'm sure your mother will like that," she said. "If she finds it too simple, we have others at different levels of difficulty."

"I'm sure she'll love it."

He looked at her and Carol felt a bit uncomfortable.

"Excuse me, ma'am," Jarmon said to Irene who had been

watching the two of them interact. "That coffee shop across the street—does it serve good coffee?"

Irene was a bit surprised by the question. "My, yes, they have very good coffee."

"Are you her boss?" he said, gesturing to Carol.

"Yes, I am."

"Is she due for a break? I'd like to take her across the street for a coffee."

"You know, now that you mention it, she is due for a break," Irene said, grinning. "Carol, why don't you take your break now?"

"I suppose I don't have anything to say about it?" Carol said.

"It's just coffee," he said.

Carol walked out with Jarmon. He put his purchase in his car, and the two of them crossed the street and entered the coffee shop. They placed their orders, took their coffees to a small table, and sat across from one another.

Jarmon took a sip from his cup. "That is good coffee. I still remember the one you made me in your kitchen."

"And you thought you had to buy me one to repay me?"

"No. I wanted to take you out for a coffee."

Carol felt herself blush. When was the last time a man asked her out—even for a coffee?

"Did you ever buy one of those coffee makers that take the pods?" she asked.

"No, I never did."

"It was a coincidence you came into the shop today, wasn't it?" she asked.

"Yes, why? What do you think?"

"I thought... I thought maybe... you are keeping an eye on me."

"Why would I do that? Did you break the law or something?"

"No. It's just that..."

"What?"

"I was thinking about Tina—"

"I almost forgot all about her. How is your friend?"

"She is still in a coma."

"That's too bad. I am sorry."

"Anyway, I was thinking you might be following me because of Tina."

"I don't see the connection. What do you mean?"

Carol paused and studied his face, looking for any sign of deception and wondering about his true motives.

"The way you questioned me at my house—you made me feel as if I had done something wrong."

"How?"

"Well, I was the last one to see Tina, and usually the last one to see a victim is the guilty party."

"Only in the movies or on TV," he said. "If I made you feel that way, then I apologize."

"Then you believe what happened to Tina was an accident."

"Yes, I do. I told you that. Why, do you have another theory?"

"Well, me and the other women in the group—our cross-stitch group—we were talking and... I really shouldn't."

"You all were thinking it was Tina's husband," he said.

Carol's mouth hung open. "How did you know? Was it him? Do you think it was him? Is Vincent a suspect?" She leaned forward, spoke quickly, and appeared quite animated.

Jarmon held up his hands. "Whoa, whoa. Don't get excited. I don't think it was him. The timeline doesn't fit. He has an unshakable alibi. He could not have arrived home before he said, and one of his neighbors witnessed him coming home around six. His 911 call was almost immediate."

Carol sat back, deflated, and stared at her coffee.

"What if—" she began.

"Don't."

"What if Vincent had an accomplice?"

"Who?"

"I don't know."

"Why?"

"Why do husbands kill wives?"

"I believe it was an accident."

"Have you looked closely at Vincent at all?"

Jarmon let out an exasperated breath. "I just wanted to take you out for a coffee. I'm not looking to solve the crime of the century."

"Sorry. I'm not trying to tell you how to do your job."

"Apology accepted."

They sat in silence for a while.

"Carol," he said. She looked at him. "Do you remember my first name?"

She nodded. "It's Mike."

He smiled. "Carol, would you like to go to dinner with me tonight?"

"I would love to, Mike."

18

Carol searched through her closet trying to decide on an outfit for dinner. It was a strange feeling; one she had not had for years. There was a fluttering in her stomach and a dizziness in her head. She looked at the clock. Mike would be here in an hour, and she hadn't chosen an outfit or done her makeup. Why was she so excited? It is no big deal, she kept telling herself. It's only dinner. She's gone out to dinner before. Not in a long time, she thought.

Carol held up two outfits. Should she wear her gray skirt or her black dress?

Carol wondered if this dinner date was a mistake. Did Mike Jarmon suspect her? Was this only a ploy to catch her in a lie? Why couldn't she just see that he was interested in her for herself? She was single, young—young enough—and still attractive. Why wouldn't he want to take her out? No reason. It shouldn't matter that Mike was a police detective and Carol was guilty of assault and leaving a seriously injured person—a friend—bleeding on her own floor.

She decided to wear the black dress.

Mike Jarmon was right on time to pick Carol up at her house. His eyes widened when she answered the door in her black dress.

"Wow, you look great!" he said.

"Thanks. Do you want to come in for a minute? I'm almost ready."

He stepped in and looked around. Nothing had changed since he was last here.

Carol stepped into her bedroom as she decided to change her earrings at the last minute. "Where are we going?" she called out.

"This place in Manchester I know."

"What is the name of it?"

"The Farm."

"The what?"

"The Farm Bar and Grille. It's great. You'll love it."

The Farm Bar and Grille was on the corner of Elm and Bridge Street, east of the river. It was on the ground floor of a three-story building with a plain brick facade. The inside was as casual as the outside with a floor of wooden boards, and brick walls.

"Would you like a table or a booth?" Mike asked Carol.

"Booth," she said.

When the menus came Mike ordered a beer and Carol white wine.

"Did your mother like the cross-stitch kit?" she asked him as they perused their menus.

"I did not plan on giving it to her until this weekend."

"What's this weekend?"

"It's her birthday."

"That's lovely. You told me your dad was gone."

"That's right. You have a good memory."

"I remember the story about that ring," she said.

Mike looked at his left hand.

Their drinks arrived and they ordered.

"Do you go out much?" Carol asked.

"Not much."

"When was the last time?"

"Longer than I care to admit."

"And you never married?"

"No. I was close a couple of times."

"What happened?"

"Once I was in too big a hurry and then realized it. The other time I was feeling desperate and that we weren't right for each other. Neither would have lasted. To have gone through with either of them would not have been fair to anyone."

"Do you think you'll ever get married?"

He smiled at her. "I don't know. Do you think I should?"

"I don't know you well enough to say one way or another. It all depends on what you want out of it."

"What did you want when you got married?"

The question caught her by surprise. Carol gave it serious thought. "That's funny, I can't exactly recall. When you're young, it's all romance and daydreaming. I focused on the little things. I remember circling our wedding day on the calendar every month like that was an accomplishment, each one a milestone."

"Wasn't it?"

She shrugged. "After a year I stopped circling the calendar."

The rest of the evening neither of them spoke of marriage again.

"How long have you been interested in cross-stitch?" he asked.

"Gee, I don't know. Almost ten years or more."

"You must like it."

She nodded.

"Why do you like it?"

Carol shrugged. "It's relaxing. There is an addictive quality to it. I come home from working two jobs and it helps me unwind. I have to focus on the work, so I forget about all my troubles."

"You have troubles?"

"Doesn't everybody?"

They sat in silence while they ate.

"Why did you want to be a police officer, Mike? And don't tell me you don't recall."

He smiled. "No, I recall, right enough." Mike paused, considering how to put into words this thing that he felt deeply in his heart. "My parents raised me with a strong sense of truth and justice. Now, I know that may sound a bit idealistic, even corny, but I don't think so. People make mistakes—God knows I've made my share and still do—but I believe it's important that when we make a mistake, we own up to it. A lot of people—a lot of people I run into in police work—try to get away with their mistakes. Usually, these mistakes cause other people harm, and these people look to someone in authority to set right the wrong that's been done to them. Does that make any sense?"

Carol stared at him open-mouthed. She felt as if he was talking about her. Did he know what she had done? Was he just toying with her, trying to get her to confess about Tina?

Just then, a couple entered the place. They were in a celebratory mood and their voices were loud. Carol was certain she knew the man's voice. She turned and there was Gary with Monica, and did they ever look happy—all smiles and laughing and very cozy. Carol felt a pang of nausea.

Gary and Monica were shown to a table where Carol could see them easily enough.

Carol and Mike were not quite done with their meal. She turned to Mike and said, "Is it okay if we go?"

"Sure," he said. "I'll go pay the check. You wait right here."

Mike returned in a minute, and he escorted her out. They walked to his car. When they were inside, she said, "I need to explain something. What happened back there... why I needed to leave."

"You don't have to explain anything," he said. "I understand."

"How could you?"

"That was your ex-husband and his new girlfriend. They just got engaged. You didn't want to stick around for that."

"How could you possibly know that?"

"I'm a trained detective, Carol. I saw how you reacted the moment they stepped into the restaurant. The woman kept looking at the diamond ring on her finger. They were very happy and mentioned champagne."

She looked at him with amazement. "I guess I couldn't keep something secret from you for long?"

"You probably could if you wanted to."

Carol wondered what he meant by that. Maybe this date was a mistake. Just one little slip and she could give herself away.

"Do you want to go for a walk along the river, or do you want me to take you home?"

She considered this. Going home was the safe bet.

"I would like to go for a nice long walk... with you."

The walk was a good choice. It was a beautiful evening. Mike was funny and thoughtful, and he didn't mind talking. Some men are quiet, and women struggle to know what they could be thinking. Carol found she enjoyed being with Mike, she enjoyed having a conversation with a man. It seemed there were so many women in her life, not that she minded, but it was good to talk with a man again.

Mike drove her home and walked Carol up to her door.

"Do you want to come in?" she asked and immediately regretted it. Even though she kept Smith Falls in a locked room, it was still a bit risky.

"No, but thanks," he said. "Today was my day off, but I work tomorrow. I would like to see you again, though, Carol."

"I would like that too, Mike."

He kissed her and said goodnight. She stood in the doorway until he drove off.

The next day Carol worked a breakfast shift at The Golden Griddle. She felt good and for some reason, her tips were more than usual. At Crafty Business, Irene wanted to know all about Carol's date with Mike Jarmon last night.

"How do you know I went on a date with him last night? I didn't tell you he asked me to dinner."

"Honey, that is the first man I've seen you talk to in quite a while, and you have been smiling and humming under your breath all afternoon. I saw the way he looked at you. Coffee in the afternoon and dinner at night—he must have it for you bad!"

Carol laughed. It felt good to know that someone had it for her bad.

"So, tell me about him," Irene said. "You wouldn't say a word when you came back from having coffee with him yesterday."

"He's just someone I met."

"How?"

"Irene!"

"Carol! How did you meet him? At the laundromat? At the grocery store? At the restaurant?"

"It was weeks and weeks ago."

"Who is he? What does he do?"

"He's a cop—okay? He is a police detective."

"A detective?" Irene said, staggered. She actually fell back a step. "How did you meet a detective? Carol, are you in trouble?"

"No! Not yet, anyway."

"How does one meet a police detective?"

"There is nothing nefarious about it, Irene. Do you remember me telling you about my friend who fell, and hit her head?"

Irene nodded. "She's in the hospital in a coma."

"Right. Well, this guy—"

"What is his name?"

"Jarmon. Mike Jarmon."

"I like that name. Go on, go on."

"He investigated my friend's accident. He came around and spoke with all the other women in the cross-stitch group. We all met the afternoon of the accident."

"Did you witness the accident?"

"What? No, we had all left before she fell."

"She fell in her own house?"

"Yes."

"How sad... and peculiar."

"What is peculiar?"

"I didn't think the police would investigate an accident in someone's home."

"Sure, they do."

"They do?"

"They did in this case."

"Do you think the police suspect foul play?"

"Foul play? What, have you been watching old Barbara Stanwyck movies?"

"No, I'm serious. People think it was an accident, but it may have been intentional."

"Okay, Nancy Drew, that's enough of that. My friend had an accident and fell. I don't want to hear any more talk about foul play. All right, Irene?"

Irene nodded. "Are you going to see him again?"

"Who? Oh, Mike Jarmon... yes, I guess. Sure. He's nice."

"Wow, 'nice', that sounds... underwhelming."

"Irene, we went out once."

"Twice if you count the coffee date."

That evening after work Carol wondered if she would get a phone call. He didn't have to ask her out tonight, just a call to ask how she was doing today, or if she had a good time last night. Maybe she should shower, in case he wanted to take her out tonight.

This was ridiculous. What was she doing? She wasn't in high school anymore. Best to do something to keep her mind off things.

Carol unlocked the door to her craft room and went in. She still had plenty of work on the cross-stitch and was intent on finishing it. She had to finish the cross-stitch. That much she understood from Agatha. It had to be completed with care and effort. No more slacking off. She would work on it every day, starting tonight. Despite the late hour, she made a coffee and went into the craft room. She turned on some music—ahh, Yo-Yo Ma—and studied the cross-stitch, planning her next section. Picking up her needle she made a stitch, then another, then another. This is how the magic of cross-stitch worked, one stitch at a time.

Since starting Smith Falls Carol had developed an efficient rhythm in her stitching. Her hand-eye coordination and the dexterity in her hands and fingers had improved.

Tonight, Carol stitched like never before. Her eyes took in every detail and her fingers moved almost instinctively, stitch after stitch. Time could not be measured and was ignored. Smith Falls became real—indeed, was real. Carol could almost hear the street sounds of Smith Falls, characters on the cross-stitch appeared to move. She swore that one of them beckoned to her.

19

This was not a dream or a nightmare, not this time. Carol knew the authentic Smith Falls. She knew the sounds and the sights, but more than that, she knew in her heart that she was in the real Smith Falls.

Carol stood in the bandstand and looked about. There was less traffic on the streets and sidewalks. Walking toward the bandstand Penelope Hope and Robert Crawford came smiling. He was dressed more casually, in a short blue jacket with light blue stripes, white trousers, and the straw hat he had chosen at the haberdashery when last they met.

Penelope wore a lovely blue and white dress that complimented his outfit. She even wore a similar straw hat, save that her hat had a blue band trimmed with a small bow and a flower. Finishing her costume was a delicate parasol and hanging from her bent elbow hung a fringed beaded bag.

Carol looked at her own costume which was a slim-fitting creme-colored dress with a matching parasol. Upon her head sat a delicate bonnet. She stepped down from the bandstand to meet her friends.

"Good day, Caroline," Penelope greeted her. "You look simply smashing!"

"Good day, Caroline," Robert repeated. "Yes, simply smashing!"

"Good day to you both."

"Are you ready for Lady Wyndemere's garden party?" Penelope asked. "We are certain you will love it."

"I am certain I will," Carol said, as she looked about expectantly.

"If you are looking for Mr. Walter Pennington, I am afraid he has been a bit delayed and said he would meet us all at the garden party as soon as he is able.

Carol nodded but could not help but feel disappointed.

"Now, now, Caroline, you mustn't look like that," Penelope said in a mild reproach. "Today is a grand day for a garden party and we insist you enjoy every minute. Now, let's see a smile. That's it. That is the Caroline I know."

"Ladies, shall we be off," Robert said, offering Carol his free arm.

Arm-in-arm the three friends walked out of the town proper and headed down the road. A little time later they came across a wonderful open area teeming with people milling about. The lawns were trimmed as were the green shrubs of roses, henna, tulsi, and jasmine. There were flowers in full bloom, such as daisies, marigolds, lilies, and asters. The arches were decorated with colorful and bountiful flowers and vines. Open tents offered copious amounts of food and drink and a place where guests could get out of the sun if they wished to. Off in the distance was a large lake where couples glided dreamily across the still surface in small rowboats and canoes. There were fountains that tinkled and from far off Carol could hear the sound of music. Everyone appeared to be having a wonderful time.

"Come," Penelope said to Carol. "You must meet our hostess, Lady Wyndemere."

There was a short line formed at the biggest and most colorful tent. Penelope and Robert led Carol to the end of the line. The waiting time did not appear long for Carol who looked about in amazement and delight at the panoramic scene, and she reveled in it all.

They had finally reached their destination. An older woman, well-dressed and adorned with pearls and diamonds sat upon a large high back chair. In her left hand, she held a lace fan which she occasionally used, then would close it with a snap. The woman had years of struggle and hardship on her face but still appeared pleasant. Every time she smiled it was only through effort and by her own indomitable will.

Penelope went first. She said hello and then thanked her hostess for inviting her. She lightly kissed the older woman on the cheek. Robert stepped forward and repeated the greeting, only he took her outstretched hand and kissed it.

Robert stepped aside revealing Carol. Lady Wyndemere cocked her head expectantly at Carol and said, "And who have we here?"

"This is our friend, Caroline," Penelope said. "I hope you do not mind that we invited her."

Lady Wyndemere gave a brief shake of her head. "Such a lovely young woman. Tell me, my dear, how is it you have no escort of your own?"

Carol was stumped at how to respond. Luckily Robert stepped in.

"Walter was to be her escort, Lady Wyndemere."

"Oh, and where is my wayward nephew?" the older woman said.

"Your nephew?" Carol almost choked on her words.

Lady Wyndemere raised her eyebrows. "Yes, and if he is your escort, he should consider himself very fortunate."

"Thank you, Lady Wyndemere," Carol said.

The woman took Carol's hand and said, "Whether my nephew attends the party or not, I want you to make it a point to enjoy yourself. I trust we will speak again." She released Carol's hand which was the signal to move off and let others greet their hostess.

Carol let Penelope and Robert lead her around. Every now and then they would stop to speak with someone and introduce Carol. Everyone appeared pleased to meet her.

"A glass of punch, ladies?" Robert suggested. They went to a tent and helped themselves to a fruit punch. Carol tasted the drink and was taken aback by the beverage, for it possessed a refreshing quality that she had never experienced. Robert had to assure her twice that there was no alcohol in the punch.

Tables under tents held a plethora of foods that were not only delicious, but their presentations were so appealing that Carol was almost content to simply look at them.

Many of the dishes were on ice, such as oysters, snails, and shrimp. There were salads; fruit salads, fresh bean salads, and leafy salads served with oil and vinegar dressing, butter and cream dressing, and mayonnaise dressing. There were platters of petit pains, petit pois, and foie gras. What was truly impressive were the desserts and sweets. Guests could choose plum pudding, plum cakes, jellies, apple puffs, strawberry tartlets, pastries, stuffed monkeys, maids of honor, peach cobbler, apple cobbler, and banana bread. There were creams served with fresh fruit. To Carol, each was a taste explosion.

There were various outdoor activities for the more ambitious such as lawn tennis and croquet. Solely for the women was an archery contest.

Penelope competed in the archery contest and Carol saw the woman was experienced, with a steady arm and a good aim. Carol and Robert cheered her on. Penelope's score was very good, but she did not win. After the competition, Penelope called Carol over to give her a lesson in archery. Penelope stood behind Carol and using her own hands showed the other woman how to grip the bow and place the arrow on the shelf rest. Penelope's hands dropped away and were replaced by the hands of a man.

Carol looked back over her shoulder with a start. She was pleasantly surprised to see Mr. Walter Pennington standing directly behind her. His arms were about her and she felt a pleasing comfort.

"Place the notch of the arrow into the bowstring," he spoke softly into her ear. "Pull back on the bowstring. Sight down the shaft of your arrow. Aim a little higher than the bullseye. Steady. Hold your breath. Take careful aim. And gently release."

Her arrow flew straight and true. It struck the target in the lower left quadrant in the black. Carol was surprised she hit the target but admitted to herself that it was more Walter's doing than her own. A small group who had gathered cheered.

"I did it!" Carol cried out and she threw her arms about him.

"Indeed, you did!" Walter said. "And a very good shot it was."

Walter Pennington wore a short burgundy jacket with ivory trim on his lapels and breast pocket. His trousers were white and, on his head, sat a light-colored Homburg with a pale band.

The four friends walk about the grounds enjoying each other's company, the scenery, and the fresh air. It was a beautiful day for a garden party.

Carol was joyful. Every visit to Smith Falls was better than the last. Each visit brought new experiences. She thought little of her home life when in Smith Falls.

The four friends played a game of croquet on the lawn. After Carol became familiar with the rules, she found she enjoyed the game and was a fairly good player.

"Are you in need of a refreshment?" Walter asked Carol.

"Not this minute."

"Walter took out his watch and checked the time. "I have not yet greeted Lady Wyndemere. She will be retiring into the house soon. Would you like to meet her?"

"I already have. When you invited me to come here, I did not know she was your aunt."

"How did you like the old girl?"

"I like her very much."

"Then come along with me. Perhaps if I am with someone, she won't berate me for not seeing her sooner."

There was no longer a line to greet Lady Wyndemere, but she was in conversation with a mature couple. They soon departed and Walter approached his aunt and kissed her lovingly on the cheek. Carol stood off to the side.

Lady Wyndemere smacked him on the arm with her fan. "Where have you been?" she said. "Do you know what time it is? It is bad enough you have kept me waiting, but you have left this lovely girl without an escort."

"Lady Wyndemere—" Carol began.

"Do not defend him, my dear," Lady Wyndemere said. "He doesn't deserve it."

Walter reached out and took Carol by the hand and drew her closer.

"What do you think of her?" he asked his aunt regarding Carol.

Lady Wyndemere looked Carol up and down approvingly. "I like her, more than I like you."

"You love me," he said. "And I love you." He leaned in and kissed her again.

She smacked him again with her fan. "I am going in," she said rising from her chair.

"Would you like us to help you?" he asked her.

"No! Do you think I'm a feeble old woman? Go on and enjoy yourselves. Caroline, I hope we meet again very soon."

"Good afternoon, Lady Wyndemere," Carol said.

The older woman gave something of a wave with her fan and walked off.

"Well, she likes you," Walter said.

"Are you surprised?"

"No. I like you too."

They walked across the lawn, arm-in-arm, but stopped when they heard someone calling Walter's name. It was Robert. He and Penelope approached the couple. Robert was carrying two tennis rackets.

"Ready for a match?" Robert said, offering one of the rackets to Walter.

The two men took to the grass court. It soon became evident they were equally good players and equally competitive. A small group of spectators soon gathered. After some lobs, droppers, and buggy whips, the game picked up the pace. Cannonballs, smashes and slices became more common. The players stopped and the two men handed their hats and jackets to their respective escorts and resumed their places on the court. By this time a large crowd had gathered and cheering and applause accompanied the match. Carol and Penelope enjoyed watching the men play. It was a close match and at the end, both shook hands in true sportsmanship.

The evening was approaching. Some guests had gone home. Walter took Carol out in a rowboat on the lake. She sat in the stern and watched him row as he smiled at her. The sun was low, but she continued to keep her parasol poised on her shoulder. Her other hand trailed in the water, and it created ripples that spread across the lake and eventually faded. Walter ceased rowing and they sat in the middle of the lake, gently bobbing on the water. The sun reflected off the surface of the lake and shone and sparkled like diamonds. An incredible feeling of peace and contentment came over Carol, and she wished the feeling would last. The sound of partygoers carried out to them over the water. How could this moment be any more perfect, she mused.

When they were on shore again, clean-up was beginning. They looked about for Penelope and Robert, but they were nowhere to be seen. Walter led Carol to a large maple tree heavily laden with foliage.

"Did you enjoy yourself?" Walter asked her. His words carried a hint that not only the garden party but also her visit was near an end.

"I had a most wonderful time," she said.

"You look tired. Why don't we sit a bit?"

They sat in the long grass beneath the tree.

"Will we two meet again?" she asked.

"Yes, of course."

"I'm so glad."

"So am I."

Carol looked about the grounds. It had been a memorable afternoon. She did not want it to end.

Walter reached over and cupped her cheek. Carol turned towards his hand and gently kissed his palm. With his fingertips, he tenderly massaged her forehead while he softly recited a poem.

Merrily we drift along,
Under the pale blue sky,
Together we sing an endless song,
My true love and I.

Let the world go its way,
Let it pass us by,
For we shall choose to live today,
My true love and I.

20

Carol opened her eyes and half expected to see Mr. Walter Pennington looking down at her. She could almost feel his fingertips caressing her forehead. Carol looked about. She was alone, of course, sitting in her craft room. She must have fallen asleep in her chair. Though the blinds were closed, she could see the morning sunlight coming in the window.

Standing up, she immediately concluded that her body took less time to climatize itself after returning from Smith Falls. Carol remembered the first time, and how nauseated she had been. She wondered if she would ever be able to cross over to Smith Falls whenever she wished. What type of force took her Smith Falls and what force brought her back? Was she destined to live in two worlds? Would there be a time when she could not return to Smith Falls? What if one day she was in Smith Falls and could never return here? If Carol had to make a choice, which would she choose? She looked at her cross-stitch and wondered what kind of power it possessed.

The next few days were pleasant for Carol as she mostly lived on the memories of Lady Wyndemere's garden party. She looked forward to coming home from her job to work on her cross-stitch. Day-by-day it grew and took shape one stitch at a time.

Amanda called. She wanted to let Carol know that, according to Vincent, Tina's condition had not changed.

"Anything new with you?" Amanda asked.

Carol thought of the garden party, which she could not mention, and then she thought of Mike Jarmon, whom she chose not to mention.

"No, nothing new with me. How about you?"

"Nothing much," Amanda said. "We'll talk again soon."

Thinking of Mike must have had some magical effect, for once Carol hung up with Amanda, he called her.

"Hello, Mike, how are you?"

"I'm good. You?"

"Good."

"I've been thinking about you."

"That's sweet. I've been thinking about you as well."

"It appears we've been doing a lot of thinking, but not

much action."

"What did you have in mind?"

"I am going to visit my mother this weekend. It's her birthday and I plan on giving her the kit you sold me. I was wondering if you wanted to come with me."

"You want me to meet your mother. Wow, you move pretty fast."

"I think you'll like her. After, we can go to dinner or a drink or something."

"I would love to meet your mother and then go to dinner or a drink or something."

They chose a time when Mike would pick her up on Sunday afternoon.

Janette Jarmon lived in a modest apartment in a modest part of Bakersville.

Carol felt nervous standing outside Mrs. Jarmon's door. Mike turned to her and gave her a smile and a wink to let her know everything was going to be fine. The door opened and they called out Happy Birthday!

Janette Jarmon greeted them with a smile and ushered the two into her apartment, which was tastefully decorated without too much clutter and a combination of older furniture and new. Mike introduced Carol and Janette took her by the hand and had her sit next to her in the small living area.

"When Michael told me he was bringing someone along I knew I had to bake something," she said, indicating the two plates of cookies. "Please, help yourself, no need to stand on ceremony. I am just so glad you are here."

The woman made Carol feel very welcome and her excitement was contagious as Carol found herself smiling and laughing readily. Mrs. Jarmon was a pleasant-looking woman in her mid-sixties with greying hair. She, of course, showed the usual physical signs of aging, but her spirit was young.

Mike handed his mother her gift which was wrapped in shiny paper with a bow.

"Carol helped me pick it out," he said.

His mother smiled at Carol and began to unwrap it. Her eyes widened as she saw what it was.

"It's a cross-stitch kit," Mike told her.

"Yes, that is what the box says."

"Have you ever done cross-stitch, Mrs. Jarmon?" Carol asked.

"No, dear, and I want you to call me Janette."

"Carol does a lot of cross-stitch," Mike said. "She's practically an expert."

"Is that so? Well, if that's the case she can get me started with this. Michael, why don't you put on some coffee or tea while Carol shows me how to do this."

Carol unpacked everything and explained what each item was. She showed Janette a cream-colored embroidery cloth—a 14-count aida cloth. The higher the count the more holes per square in. A 14-count is good for beginners.

"We take the cloth and stretch it on the six-inch hoop. When handling the cross-stitch, we should always make certain our hands are clean. Also, we are going to need a good pair of scissors."

"Michael," Janette called out. "Bring me my scissors from the junk drawer in the kitchen."

Carol showed Janette the rich dark red floss that came in the kit. "This is our floss or thread. We're going to cut a length of thread—about the length of your hand to your elbow. If the length is too long it makes it difficult to handle, especially at the beginning, and if it is too short you'll run out of floss too soon. We cut the floss and then we have to separate two strands. We put these strands aside and we're going to thread the two stands. First, we must separate them so there are no knots or twists in the floss.

"This kit comes with three needles, all nickel-plated, and the eye of each needle is 18 karat gold-plated."

"18 karat gold-plated!" repeated Janette. "Oh, Michael, this must have been very expensive! Why did you spend so much?"

"It didn't cost as much as you think, mum."

"The gold plating makes it easier to thread the needle," Carol said. "Now, I bet you know how to thread the needle. Here is the needle and here are the two strands of floss, so we simply thread the floss in the eye. Yes, just like that. Now we pull it through the eye only about four inches. Now we have a short end and a long end."

Carol showed Janette how to start to stitch from the back of the cloth, make a few stitches while holding down the end of the thread, and then anchor the loose end with some stitches.

"This way you won't have to keep holding down the loose end," Carol said. "Now there are many types of stitches, but I want you to focus on a cross stitch, like the ones I made. Try to always make your stitches the same. If you start on your stitch on the upper right to the lower left, then you cross that stitch by going from upper left to lower right, try to make all your cross-stitches like that. That way your stitches will be consistent and look the same."

"How do I stitch a picture?" Janette wanted to know.

"We will concentrate on the pattern a bit later. For now, it's important to just practice your stitches."

As Janette practiced her stitches, Carol said to her, "You know what you might wish to do is join or form a cross-stitch group."

"What do you mean?"

"If there are other women—or even men, for that matter—in your building who cross-stitch, you might want to form a cross-stitch group where you all can get together regularly and work on your projects. You can rotate where the group can meet. I think it would be good for you. It is a great chance to meet new people and form friendships built on a common interest."

"Do you belong to a cross-stitch group?" Janette asked.

"Why, yes, I do."

"I suppose I couldn't join your group?"

Carol paused and looked at Mike, who shrugged.

"I could ask the other women if they would be open to a new member," Carol said.

"How would you get to their meeting, Mum?" Mike asked. "You don't have a car."

"Couldn't you give me a ride?"

"I suppose I could," he said.

"Or I could," Carol said.

"Would you?"

"Well... sure."

"Let's take this slow, Mum. After all, you just made your first stitch."

"This was your idea, Michael. You bought it for me."

"I should have known this would come back on me," he said with a grin.

It was a very pleasant afternoon, and Carol was glad she came. She liked Mike's mother and enjoyed her company.

"I want to show you something before you go," Janette said to Carol. "You stay here." She got up, went into another room, and came back carrying a framed picture. Janette sat next to Carol and showed her the photograph. "This is Michael when he was four years old."

"Oh, he was adorable," Carol said smiling and looking at Mike.

"He was," Janette agreed. "People would comment what a good-looking boy he was." She looked at her son. "I still think he's good-looking."

Carol looked at him. "So do I."

The conversation never stopped, and time went by unnoticed until Mike looked at his watch, and said, "I think it's time to go."

"What?" Janette said, clearly disappointed. "Always coming and going. Kids today."

"Kids? Mum, I'm forty," Mike said, then turning to Carol said, "I just need to go to the washroom."

Janette took Carol's hand. "I am so glad you came. I hope you come again. I can tell you're someone special. Michael hasn't brought a woman to see me in years."

The two women were saying goodbye and hugging when Mike came back.

"So, where are you two off to?" Janette asked.

"We're going to grab a bite to eat," he said.

"Janette, would you like to join us?" Carol asked.

"Oh, no, thank you. I have something prepared. I just have to heat it up. You two go and enjoy yourselves."

In the car, Mike asked Carol, "Do you like Thai food?"

"I've never had it, but I am willing to try."

"Great. I know of a nice place that's close by."

After they ordered they sat in silence for a time.

"I really liked meeting your mother. She's great," Carol said.

"I shouldn't be surprised that you two hit it off," he said.

"She…" Carol started to say something but was overcome with a thought that stunned her into silence. Only now did she see the similarity between meeting Mike's mother and Carol's encounter with Lady Wyndemere. Both women were alike in some ways and Carol had liked them both very much. The two older women appeared to like her as well. How did she not see this earlier? Did it mean something? So preoccupied with this concept, that she was not aware that Mike was saying her name.

"Carol, Carol. Are you okay? Are you all right, honey?" he asked. His face looked very concerned. "Carol, what's wrong?"

"What? Oh, nothing. I was just thinking."

"You looked like you were in a trance. Like you were in another world. What were you thinking about?"

"Uhm… I was… thinking about my cross-stitch group."

"Your cross-stitch group?" He sounded unconvinced.

"I was telling your mother about joining or forming a group and she asked about mine. Just now I was thinking about poor Tina and wondered if she would ever come back to the group."

"Carol, I'm sorry. I didn't mean… I'm sorry. Do you want to stay, or…"

She reached across the table and laid her hand on his.

"No, I'm fine. I would like to stay."

Carol enjoyed her Thai dish, though she did need her water glass refilled regularly.

"It is okay that I don't finish it?" she asked Mike.

"You didn't like it."

"No, I liked it. It's just that there is so much of it."

"We can box it and you can take it home."

"You know what I think might work better. Why don't we box it, and you can take it home."

"Wow. Finishing your meal. That is a big step in a relationship. I don't know if I'm ready for that."

"I think you can handle it."

After the restaurant, Mike took Carol home and walked her to her door.

"I want to kiss you goodnight," he said.

"I want you to kiss me goodnight."

It was a long, lingering kiss that neither of them wanted to end.

When it did end, she asked him, "Do you want to come in?"

"Yes, but I won't," he said reluctantly. "I don't want to rush it. We have time. I think I love you."

Carol grew weak in the knees and hoped she wouldn't collapse.

Mike kissed her again. "Goodnight, Carol."

"Goodnight."

Carol went into her house, and she felt like singing. She felt like dancing. It was good to be alive. That is how she felt now—like she was fully alive. This was life-changing, she thought. This
was big in her life.

She poured herself a drink and unlocked the door of her craft room. She went inside and looked at her cross-stitch. Carol had studied the work to a point where it felt like she knew every stitch. How long ago had she stitched that bandstand, she thought. The bandstand wasn't complete, she knew. None of it was. Once she had stitched every figure, every building, horse, tree, and whatever, they would all have to be backstitched.

Carol looked at the character she knew was Mr. Walter Pennington.

"Oh, my goodness!" she exclaimed, smacking a palm to her forehead. "What a slow-witted fool I am!"

She had been slow to see the similarity between meeting Mrs. Jarmon and her meeting Lady Wyndemere, but this was beyond slow. How did she not see this?

As difficult as this was to believe, Carol suddenly realized she was in love with two men—Walter Pennington and Mike Jarmon!

Oh, you fool, she berated herself. How could this have happened? She was in love with two different men from two different worlds. This was not your typical love triangle, and it did not bode well. This was a big problem. The entire situation could end in disaster. What was she going to do?

21

Carol did not know how to sort out her problem. Two different men from two different worlds. She considered making a chart with two columns—Mike and Walter. She would list their pros and cons. Maybe a Venn diagram would be better.

She decided to try to sort it out in her head.

Walter Pennington was handsome and charming, a true gentleman with old-world manners. He recited poetry to her and when she was with him it was like living a dream. Smith Falls was a dream world, romantic and so different than her life here. When she was there with Walter, she believed that was where she was destined to live, where she longed to be. Walter had charming friends and was the nephew of Lady Wyndemere. How could life with Walter be more perfect?

Det. Mike Jarmon on the other hand was also handsome and charming, not in an old-world way, but in the present-day way. Carol liked his mother very much. He had a very interesting job. Carol did not even know if Walter had a job. Maybe he was independently wealthy living off Lady Wyndemere. Mike being a police detective has its downside. It can be a dangerous job, but it could also be dangerous for Carol. What if he ever discovered Carol's role in Tina's accident? How could she stay with Mike and continue to keep that secret from him? What if they ever married and she would have to keep this secret from him for the rest of her life? Maybe Mike Jarmon's interest in Carol was just a cover to discover that very truth. Carol couldn't believe that. Mike also was here, in the present-day world—the real world. But was Smith Falls less real than this world? In some ways, it was just as real. Who would pass up an opportunity to live in Smith Falls? For most people on the planet, this world was all they knew. Most never even suspected other worlds existed, let alone actually visit one as Carol had, and probably will again. Would she have to choose, she wondered. Would she be able to exist in both worlds going back and forth with one love in this world and another in Smith Falls? Wouldn't it be like living two lives—having two lifetimes when others get only one? Or would she have to decide on one world? If she had to decide—which life would she choose?

These thoughts were almost too much for her. Her mind whirled and began to ache. Suddenly, she felt tired. Carol dreaded the thought of the day that Tina would come out of her coma and tell everyone it was Carol who caused her fall. How could Carol explain why she did not call for an ambulance? She certainly could not say it was Tina's fault for stealing the chart of an enchanted cross-stitch that no one is supposed to know about.

Her phone rang. Carol answered.

"Hi, this is Wendy Hillier, Mammoth Real Estate, how are you today? Is this Carol?"

"Yes."

"How are you, Carol?"

"Good."

"As you know, Carol, I'm the agent that will be handling the sale of the house."

"Yes." Carol pressed her hand to her forehead in hopes of keeping her head from exploding. With everything that had happened, Carol completely forgot that Gary said she would be contacted about the house.

"Carol, can we set up a time for me to see the inside of the house?"

"I suppose."

"How about right now?"

"Now? How soon can you get here?"

"I'm standing by the curb."

Carol went to the window and saw a young blonde-haired woman leaning against an expensive sports car talking on the phone. The woman waved to her.

"Yes, I guess right now would be all right."

"Fantastic!"

Carol opened the front door. On a closer look, she saw that Wendy Hillier was slim in a matching jacket and skirt and was quite attractive. She could almost be a model. Carol, on the other hand, had no makeup, was dressed in pajamas, and hadn't even combed her hair.

"Carol, nice to meet you, I'm Wendy Hillier, Mammoth Real Estate," Wendy said, giving Carol first a professional handshake and then her business card. "I just took a picture of the house from the curb for the listing. If you want to tidy up the front some more, I can come back and take another. My, this is a lovely home."

My, this is a lovely home, must have been the first line they taught in real estate school.

"Can I see the interior, then the backyard?"

"Can I offer you a drink—coffee?"

"No, thank you, I've already had two this morning."

Carol suspected Wendy was a bit hyped up on caffeine.

As Carol escorted the woman through the house, she repeated, "Excuse the mess."

"Don't worry about any mess right now," Wendy said. "I have seen some true disasters. But when we show the house, it would be best if it looked as neat and clean as possible. It has to be appealing to buyers."

They went past the craft room and Wendy tried the doorknob. "It's locked," she said, with an inquisitive look. "Do you keep this locked for a reason?"

Carol had completely forgotten about the craft room. "I must have locked it by accident."

"Is it a bedroom?"

"Yes, I recently converted it to my craft room."

"Oh, you do crafts. What crafts do you do?"

"Mostly cross-stitch."

"Can we see the room?"

"Of course. Can you give me a minute?"

Carol let herself in and closed the door on Wendy. She considered taking the cross-stitch out of the floor stand and tucking it in the closet. She decided to simply get a light throw from the closet and drape it over the work. Taking the cross-stitch chart, she tucked it under the chair cushion. She opened the door and had Wendy come in.

"Everything good?" Wendy said.

"Yes."

"This is a nice room. It must be the smallest bedroom. Is it the smallest?"

Carol nodded.

"It makes a very nice craft room. Is this what you're working on?" Wendy asked as she reached to lift the throw.

Immediately Carol placed her hand on hers to keep her from revealing the cross-stitch.

"I really don't like showing my work until it's completed. You understand."

Wendy raised her eyebrows and made a questioning face.

"Oooo-kay," Wendy said.

They exited the room and Wendy turned to Carol. "When

showing the house, this room should be kept unlocked and open so even if buyers don't step inside, at least they can look in. You understand. Fantastic!"

Carol nodded. She showed Wendy the rest of the house and the backyard. Wendy asked for a glass of water and sat at the kitchen table making notes.

"So can we arrange for an open house this weekend?" Wendy proposed.

"So soon?"

"The sooner the better."

"Yes, I suppose this weekend would work."

"So, you believe you will have everything in order by then?"

What Carol believed she meant by that was, Are you going to have this place cleaned up by then?

"Yes, everything will be in order by then," Carol said, almost mechanically.

"Fantastic! And that door will not be locked."

"No."

"Fantastic! When I learn a buyer is interested in seeing the house, I will contact you as soon as possible. Would you be comfortable giving me a key to the house in case you are not home?"

"No, I don't think so."

Wendy looked at Carol as if to say, Are you sure you don't want to change your mind?

"No," Carol repeated.

"Oooo-kay."

Wendy stood up and collected her things. "You have my card, and I will be in touch. You know, Carol, when you start thinking about moving to another place—I don't know what your plans are—but if you're thinking about another place, give me a call and I can help."

Carol nodded, but she had no intention of calling Wendy.

"Just so you know, Carol, my position is this; there is a job to do, let's work together and get the job done. Agreed?

Fantastic!"

Wendy Hillier was out the door and drove off faster than Carol could say Fantastic!

Carol felt tired just being around that woman.

It was only then Carol realized that she was hosting the cross-stitch group this afternoon and she had a lot to prepare.

22

Carol looked in the kitchen and saw she had nothing to serve her guests. She made a quick trip to the store and bought some items. A few bottles of wine were on her list. When she arrived home, she started to clean up, especially the living room where they met, the kitchen, and the bathroom. The rest of the house would have to wait. The craft room would remain locked.

Carol had just showered and changed when Harriet and Margaret arrived. She greeted them with a smile and invited them inside. Soon Amanda arrived and announced, "I feel the itch, the itch to stitch!"

With the group complete they all settled in and began on their projects.

"Has anyone heard anything about Tina?" Harriet asked.

"No change," Amanda said. "I make regular calls to Vincent, and he assures me there has been no change."

Carol wanted to say that she would not believe anything Vincent said, but she remained silent.

Everyone went quiet for a few minutes, each one thinking of Tina. Every cross-stitch meeting was like a remembrance day of her fateful accident.

"And how is everything with you, Carol?" Harriet asked.

"Good. Oh, and just to let you all know, this will likely be the last meeting here in this house. The real estate agent was here today. I'm surprised she didn't leave a sign on the lawn. I doubt a sign could fit in that sports car."

"What was she like?" Amanda asked.

"I think she does pretty well... with male customers, anyway," said Carol.

"Oh? One of those types?" Harriet said.

"She was all right I guess," Carol conceded. "Everyone has to make a living."

"Any idea where you are going to go?" asked Harriet.

"I'll have to start looking," Carol said, thoughtfully. "Most likely an apartment. I'll have to sell most of the furniture. Of course, half of it belongs to Gary."

"Do you think he'll want it?" Amanda asked.

"If he doesn't, he is entitled to half of what it sells for."

"What are you working on, Carol?" Margaret asked.

Carol turned her Flowers in a Vase cross-stitch toward Margaret, who got up from her seat and came over for a closer look.

"Have you not worked on that since last time?" Margaret asked a bit confused. "It doesn't look like you added a stitch. Have you been working on something else—Smith Falls, perhaps?"

Carol could not get over this woman's eye for detail. Of course, she hadn't worked on Flowers in a Vase. All her cross-stitch time had gone to Smith Falls, but she couldn't admit it. Carol tried to remember if she locked that craft room door.

"No, I put that one away," Carol lied. "The truth is I haven't had much time to stitch."

"No?" Margaret said as if she did not believe her. Margaret went back to her chair.

"Why is that, dear?" asked Harriet.

Carol shrugged. "Just too busy."

"Doing what?" Amanda asked.

Carol felt the walls closing in on her. She did not realize her friends were so nosey. Better diffuse this quickly.

"You'll never guess who came into Crafty Business the other day," Carol said.

Everyone paused, but no one said, 'Who?'

"Det. Mike Jarmon."

"What?" they all said together. Shock and questions ran through the room.

"Are you kidding?"

"What was he doing there?"

"What did you do?"

"Are you serious?"

"What did he want?"

Carol almost smiled that she had so successfully changed the subject.

"It was just a coincidence, and he came to buy his mother a gift," Carol said. "He bought her a cross-stitch kit."

"Did you talk to him?" Amanda asked.

"I waited on him. I helped him pick out the kit."

Everyone laughed, even Margaret.

"Did he remember you?" Harriet asked. "He must have recognized you. Did he?"

"Oh, he did," Carol said.

"What happened?" Margaret finally asked a question.

"We went out for coffee on my break."

There was a string of exclamations. Everyone laughed.

"What's he like?" Amanda wanted to know.

"He's nice."

"I can't believe this," Harriet said.

"That night he took me out to dinner."

The room erupted again in laughter and questions.

"Now I know you're making this up," Amanda said.

Carol shook her head. "We went to the Farm Bar and Grille on Elm."

"This is unbelievable," Harriet said.

"On Sunday, he took me to meet his mother."

"Noooooo!" filled the room.

"Wow, that guy works fast!" Amanda exclaimed. "He took you to meet his mother!"

"She's very nice. I gave his mother her first cross-stitch lesson. She would like to join our group."

"Carol, you cannot be serious!" Amanda said.

"I am totally serious. How does everyone feel about a new group member?"

The room went silent as they tried to process all of Carol's revelations.

"So, should I bring her to our next meeting?"

"You're serious," Harriet said.

"I think everyone would like her. I like her."

"Do we have to decide today?" Amanda asked.

"No, but we should decide before the next meeting," Carol said. "By the way, who has the next meeting?"

Margaret raised her hand.

"If everyone can get back to me in a week or two, I can let her know."

"What's her name?" Harriet asked.

"Janette. Janette Jarmon."

"J.J.," Amanda said. "That's cute."

The rest of the meeting was taken up by more questions about Mike Jarmon, Tina, Harriet's flowers, and the usual gossip and conversation. Once in a while, they even talked about cross-stitch."

It was a good meeting, but Carol was relieved when everyone left.

Carol had cleaned up and sat down with a drink when her phone rang. It was Harriet.

"Hello, Harriet, did you forget something?" Carol said.

"No. I just wanted to thank you for hosting today. It was a good meeting, don't you think?"

"Yes, it was very good."

"You just shocked everyone today when you brought up Det. Jarmon."

"Yes, I know."

"Listen, Carol, I was thinking about your living accommodations and that you'll have to move out of your house. I didn't want to bring this up in front of the others in case it embarrassed you, but I was thinking, I have a big house, bigger than I need. I don't want to sell it. I've lived here forever."

"What are you trying to say, Harriet?"

"You could move in here with me... if you want... if you think that would help."

"Gee, Harriet, that is a very kind offer, but I wouldn't want to put you out."

"You wouldn't be putting me out. Not at all."

"Thank you, Harriet, I..."

"You don't have to decide today, and it doesn't have to be permanent. Take some time and think about it."

"All right, Harriet, I'll think about it."

23

A house sign went up on Carol's lawn the next day, and every day Carol would have to look at Wendy Hillier's smiling face. There were two open houses on the weekend. Carol avoided the one on Saturday by taking a shift at the Golden Griddle and Crafty Business. Sunday, she spent the time with Mike Jarmon. They went to see his mother and Carol gave her another cross-stitch lesson. Both days Carol tucked away the Smith Falls cross-stitch in the back of the closet.

One evening Mike and Carol went out for dinner. He never took her to one of the more elegant restaurants in Manchester, like The Birch or Hanover Street, but Carol didn't mind.

"You might be happy to know that I've taken your advice," Mike told her as they sat before their meal in the restaurant.

"My advice? What advice is that?"

"To take a closer look at Vincent DeLuca."

Carol almost choked on her food.

"Are you okay?" he asked concerned. "Drink some water."

She did. Mike got up and went to her side prepared to give her a few good slaps on the back. She appeared not to need any, so he sat back down.

"When did I say that?" she asked, with a cough.

"When did you say what?"

"That you should take a closer look at Vincent DeLuca."

"When we first went out for coffee. You remember."

"Oh yeah. Now I remember."

"So, I started to look into the possibility that DeLuca may have taken part in his wife's accident."

"And did you find anything?"

"Carol, what I'm about to tell you is in the strictest of confidence. Now, I trust you, but you must swear not to tell anyone—not the women in your cross-stitch club, not my mother, not anyone." He looked at her expectantly.

Carol was in a bit of a shock, and she could only stare back. She soon realized Mike was waiting for some response from her.

"I promise," she said. He looked at her like he needed more. She raised her right hand. "I swear not to tell anyone."

He nodded. "Vincent has an ironclad alibi, that's for sure. I checked it out thoroughly. Your idea that Vincent may have had an accomplice gave me an idea, so I decided to check it out." Mike paused for dramatic effect.

"Well, tell me. Did you find something? You found something. What did you find?"

He smiled at her anxiousness. "Vincent has a girlfriend on the side."

"No!"

"Yes. I've seen them together. You didn't know about this, did you?"

"Me? How would I know? Do you think I've nothing better to do than stake out Vincent DeLuca's house and follow him around?"

"No. I was simply thinking that women talk. Maybe Tina said something at one of your meetings."

"You make them sound like we go to A.A."

"Well, when you get together it's therapeutic, isn't it?"

"Yes, I suppose."

"There's a lot of talking and sharing in the group, isn't there?"

"Oh, yeah. Lots of talking."

"The conversations are confidential, aren't they?"

"Mostly," Carol paused in thought. "Funny, I never thought of our cross-stitch group quite like that."

"So, Tina never alluded to her husband having an affair?"

She shook her head. "No, she never. I don't know if she is the type of person to admit something like that. Tina is a perfectionist. She wouldn't admit not being perfect, not even in her marriage."

They ate in silence for a short time.

"So, who is this sweet thing Vincent has on the side? Someone from work?"

Mike shook his head. "No, a married neighbor down the street from him."

"What?" Carol almost yelled. Her exclamation started another choking spasm. Patrons in the restaurant turned their heads in her direction. Mike was at her side again gently smacking her on the back. She realized that was an unwarranted overreaction. She would have to be more careful.

"Are you all right, now?" Mike asked her.

Carol nodded her head, and he took his seat.

"What was that?" he asked, referring to her sudden outburst.

"You just surprised me, that's all."

I had already told you Vincent was having an affair, but you're shocked it's with his neighbor?"

Carol sat back and took a few deep breaths to relax.

"I am just in shock. This is all so upsetting," she said.

"I'm sure it is. All this and you have to sell your house."

"How do you know that?"

"I saw the sign on your lawn, Carol. It's not hard to figure out."

There was more eating in silence.

"So, what do you plan to do about Vincent?" Carol asked quietly.

"Just to watch him for now. I don't have any evidence that Tina's fall was anything more than an accident. It may have been staged to look like one, but I don't know. I can't arrest a guy for having an affair, but so far, that is all I can prove."

Carol should have been glad. If Vincent was accused of causing Tina's fall, it would not be long before he brought up the thing about the slippers and how Carol was the last one known to be with Tina. She wondered when this nightmare would ever end. Smith Falls was looking pretty good to Carol right now.

All this seemed to sour the evening for Carol. After dinner, she asked Mike to take her home. They were both quiet in the car. Mike did not speak until they were standing at Carol's doorstep.

"I think I ruined our dinner with shop talk," he said. "I should have never brought up the subject."

"No. It wasn't your fault. There is just so much happening."

"Can I call you?"

"I'll call you," she said. They exchanged goodnights, but that was all.

The next day Carol felt an overwhelming need—that likely stemmed from guilt— to return to the hospital to see Tina. Once there she first went to the gift shop. She asked the young girl at the counter if she knew what they would allow in a patient's room who was in the ICU. The girl told her that plush toys were allowed, and she showed Carol a nice assortment. Carol picked out a small white teddy bear holding a heart-shaped sign that read Hope. This was as appropriate as anything in the shop. There was a small, folded gift card tied to the bear's ear. After purchasing the teddy bear, Carol took a pen and poised thinking about what to write. *Tina, I'm sorry.* She needed something more and wrote *I…* She struggled to finish the note. All she could think of was, *I'm so, so sorry. – Carol.*

Carol rode the elevator up to the Intensive Care Unit. Instead of sneaking into Tina's room like last time, Carol decided to be more honest and go to the nursing station. There she inquired about Tina DeLuca. She spoke with a very nice nurse about her age, who told her Tina could only have guests in the room if they were a blood relation. Again, Carol practiced honesty and said that she was not a relative, but that Tina was her friend. When she asked the nurse regarding Tina's current condition, the nurse regrettably said that the family—meaning Vincent—requested her condition be kept confidential.

"Can I leave this for her?" Carol asked and put the teddy bear on the counter.

The nurse, like all nurses, was a sympathetic person, and she said, "I'll run this right in there. I can't stop you from following me up to her door."

Carol followed the nurse and stood at the door to Tina's room. Everything looked exactly the same as when she was there previously. Tina lay still in the bed with tubes coming out of her and the machines hummed. The nurse put the teddy bear near the bed. Carol nodded to the nurse in thanks and walked away.

When she arrived home from the hospital, Carol got a call from Janette Jarmon.

"Hello, Carol, dear, how are you?"

"I'm good Janette. How are you?"

"Oh, I'm fine. I hope you don't mind me calling you. I got your number from Michael. What do you want it for? He asked. None of your business, I told him. It's something concerning women. He didn't ask any more after that."

"No, I don't mind you calling. Is it about joining our group?"

"No, unless a decision had been made. Has it?"

"I'm afraid not yet. I told the other ladies to think about it and get back to me as soon as possible."

"The reason I called was because I think I'm ready to move on with the cross-stitch. I have been practicing the stitches and I want to move on to making the picture. Is there some time you might be able to come over and help me along?"

"Certainly, Janette, how about today?"

"Are you sure, dear? You're not too busy?"

"No. I could be there in no time."

"Well, that would be just wonderful. Thank you."

Carol threw some things in a bag and drove over to Janette's apartment.

Janette greeted her warmly and showered her in thanks. They sat and Janette showed Carol her stitches.

"Very good," Carol said. "I can see the difference from the first ones you did here, and how much better they look at the end. You are going to do just fine. Now, the first thing we'll do is get rid of these stitches and start fresh."

"Can't we use these? Some of them are good."

Carol smiled at this. "No, we'll start fresh. Now the first thing we will do is some frogging to these stitches."

"Frogging?"

"Frogging is when you have to pop out stitches because you made an error. Let's say you put the wrong color or the wrong stitch in a row before you realize you made a mistake and have to remove them all. Just use a seam ripper. I'm sure you have one in your sewing kit. If you don't, I believe I have one in my bag."

"Why do they call it frogging?" Janette asked.

Carol took up the cross stitch and with the seam ripper, she began ripping the stitches.

"Do you hear the sound it makes? It sounds like a frog, rip-it... rip-it."

Janette laughed. Janette repeated the phrase, rip-it, rip-it, and this caused Carol to laugh. Every once in a while during their time together, one of them would say, rip-it, rip-it, which would induce another bout of laughter.

One of the patterns that came with the kit was a pastel rainbow heart. Carol thought this was good for a beginner. Carol had Janette thread her needle and then showed her where to start for the work to be centered.

"Now that you have chosen your starting point, thread the needle through the back, I know you can do that. We stitch from left to right. Now follow the chart and count how many stitches you have to make."

Carol thought Janette would make a good cross-stitcher. Janette eagerly showed her first row of stitches to Carol for inspection.

"Now before you anchor the end, we will just double-check the number of stitches," Carol said and counted the stitches on the chart and then on the cloth.

"I believe you made one stitch too many," she said.

"Is that important?"

"We must strive for perfection in cross-stitch."

"Should I frog them out?"

"No," said Carol smiling. She showed Janette how to remove the stitch.

Janette carried on with her stitching. "It is a shame we cannot remove our mistakes in life as easily as we can remove mistakes from a cross-stitch."

Carol looked at her and was taken by her statement.

"Have you made many mistakes in your life that you would like to remove?" Carol asked her.

"Honey, I think we all make mistakes we wish we could remove."

"So…"

"So what?" Janette asked.

"So, what's the answer? What do we do about our mistakes?"

Janette shrugged, as she kept her eyes on her stitching. "We own up to our mistakes. We admit it, learn from them, and make amends if we can."

Carol was hoping for more than that. She was hoping for some kind of resolution to her problem regarding Tina, but it was not going to be that easy.

While Janette worked on her first cross-stitch, Carol worked on her Flowers in a Vase. As was typical when women came together to cross-stitch and talk, time was insignificant.

The two women were interrupted by a knock on the door. Janette answered it and her son Mike stepped in. He hugged his mother and saw Carol sitting there cross-stitching.

"I came to surprise my mum, and here I get surprised!" he said. Turning to Carol he said, "What are you doing here?" He tried to make the question sound friendly, but it wasn't entirely convincing.

"What does it look like we're doing here?" Janette said. "We're cross-stitching."

"Do you two know what time it is?" Mike asked.

Janette looked at the clock on the wall. She touched Carol's arm. "It's almost six."

"Oh, my," said Carol. "I had no idea."

"Come on, you two. I'm taking you out for dinner," Mike said.

They ended up in a nice family restaurant close by. Mike was quiet, but Janette never let the conversation fade out. She loved to talk and was very good at it. Every once in a while, Janette would repeat the phrase rip-it, rip-it, and the two women would giggle. Mike simply shook his head.

After dinner, Mike took the two women back to Janette's and Carol packed up her stuff. When she bid Janette goodnight, Mike said he had to leave too. He walked Carol to her car.

"Do you want to go for a drink?" he asked her.

"How about some other time," she said.

"I have something to tell you."

"Okay. Tell me."

"I think you're going to want a drink."

They went to a bar close to the river and sat at a small

table in the corner. He ordered a whiskey sour and she a glass of white wine. They got their drinks.

"Is this about Vincent DeLuca?" Carol asked.

"Partly."

"Is it about Vincent's girlfriend?"

"No, it's about Vincent's wife."

"Tina? What about Tina? Did she come out of her coma?"

The last question she attempted to ask with concern in her voice, not with dread.

Mike shook his head. "I don't believe she'll ever come out of her coma."

"What do you mean?"

"You are going find out all about this eventually, but you can't tell anyone that I told you."

"What?"

"I was able to talk to a nurse in the ICU. She told me this in confidence, so I'm swearing you to confidence."

He waited for Carol to acknowledge this. She did, and he continued.

"Soon after Tina was admitted, she was diagnosed with PCU—post-coma unresponsiveness."

She instinctively took a drink of her wine and stared at him across the table. "What does that mean?"

"It means she suffered brain damage and was in—what they call—a disorder of consciousness."

"But she opened her eyes!"

"They call that a state of partial arousal. She was later diagnosed with PVS—persistent vegetative state, which is another way of saying permanent vegetative state."

Carol took another drink.

"Permanent," she repeated under her breath. "You mean Vincent knew all this and never once told us. He purposely kept us in the dark."

"That's not the only thing," Mike said, and he took a drink. "The nurse told me that Vincent DeLuca had been inquiring about euthanasia. I think he wants to pull the plug on his wife."

Carol sat and stared in shock. She didn't know how to feel. Though they had never been close friends, Carol had known Tina for years and were in the same cross-stitch group. Carol would now be partly responsible for Tina's death. Carol's actions had led to the death of another human being. She felt sick. But her rational mind told her, Tina's death would forever keep her secret from being revealed. Even if Tina were to remain brain-dead, that would practically guarantee Carol's safety. She had to admit that this latest revelation changed everything.

24

Carol did not stay long at the bar. A wave of sickness overcame her. It wasn't just the nausea in the belly she sometimes would get. This was an all-encompassing soul sickness that was exhibited with overwhelming feelings of hopelessness, and helplessness. There was a perceived sense of incompetence and demoralization that invaded every fiber of her being. When Carol drove away from the bar her hands were shaking, and her head swam dizzily. She should not have been driving. At one point she had the awareness to pull to the side of the road. Opening the door, she turned to the left and vomited. Carol waited for this awful feeling to subside, but it did not. When she thought she was well enough to drive with relative safety, she continued on home.

At home, Carol went to her bed and laid down in a fetal position. She was still fully dressed, but she pulled the covers over her.

In the morning Carol had no intention of getting out of bed, but it was either that or soil her sheets. Coming out of the bathroom she saw by the clock that it was late. She had slept the morning away. She had missed her shift at the

Golden Griddle and was due at Crafty Business. Carol managed to call Irene and tell her she was sick and could not come in today. What Irene said she barely heard. Carol went back to bed. During the afternoon her phone rang several times, but she did not answer.

Sleep—she just wanted to sleep. Her body ached with weariness and pain. It was a weariness borne out of life's totality and the pain that plagued her was beyond any earthly pain, for it seemed to come from the soul of the universe. Perhaps if she slept, the pain and weariness would go away. She so wanted it all, all to go away. She drifted off secure that sleep would lend her some respite from her suffering.

Carol found herself sitting on a bench within sight of the bandstand. Even sitting here on the bench, Carol felt content just to sit and watch the world here in Smith Falls go by. She turned, and sitting next to her was her friend Penelope Hope.

"Did you enjoy the garden party, Caroline," her friend asked.

Carol recalled Lady Wyndemere's garden party and how lovely it was.

"Oh, yes, very much."

"I'm so glad. Her Ladyship is having a ball at her house, and we are all invited. Doesn't that sound wonderful?"

"Yes, wonderful," Carol said, but there was little joy in her words.

They continued to sit there in silence. Two young boys ran by each pursuing a hoop with a stick. The women smiled at this. More silence.

"You appear upset by something, Caroline. Is there something wrong? Is something troubling you?"

"No… yes. Something is troubling me. I feel that there is an important decision I must make, and I need to make the right decision."

"I'm certain you will make the right decision, Caroline."

"But how do you know?"

Penelope looked down in thought.

"Have you ever considered, Caroline, the importance of our names?"

"I beg your pardon."

"Our names. My name is Penelope, which means desired child, life, and strength. Your name, Caroline, means strong, and free woman. I believe you are strong enough and free enough to make your own choice of who you want to be, and where you want to live. You have the ability to make these choices."

"Do you truly believe that, Penelope?"

"I wish you could see yourself the way I and others see you."

Caroline looked away and her friend intuited her dilemma.

"Let not your heart be troubled, Caroline. Everyone here loves you."

"They do?"

"Of course, they do. Robert and myself, Mr. Walter Pennington, Lady Wyndemere. Everyone who has met you loves and cares for you."

"But none of you know—"

"Caroline," Penelope cut her off, "it doesn't matter what you've done or who you were. Here, you are loved."

Carol tried to grasp this. It was so unlike anything she was familiar with. She tried to reason it out.

"Penelope," she asked, hesitantly, "is this heaven?".

Penelope smiled. "Heaven? My dear Caroline, this is Smith Falls."

Carol was roused by the sound of persistent knocking on her front door. She had no intention of getting up and seeing who it was. Strangely enough, the knocking ceased to be replaced by a call of hello. Someone was in the house calling out her name. She was afraid that she knew that voice.

"Carol, are you all right?"

Carol looked up and saw Wendy Hillier standing at the

door of her bedroom. Seeing the real estate agent, Carol let out a moan.

Wendy came to her bedside. "Carol, are you ill?" Wendy felt her forehead. "Can I get you anything? Do you want me to call someone for you?"

At each question, Carol would shake her head.

"Listen, I am going to go into the kitchen and see if I can fix you some soup," Wendy said, kindly. She adjusted the blanket and tucked Carol in. "You stay right here."

Carol could hear Wendy talking on her phone in another room. Several minutes later Wendy returned with hot soup and crackers, a cup of coffee, and buttered bread. She had Carol sit up and insisted that Carol eat. Carol went through the motions, all the while embarrassed at the woman's kindness, and her former opinion of Wendy.

"I've been calling and calling," Wendy said gently. "I did not know if you were at work, but I took the chance you might be home. Seeing your car in the driveway, I knocked but there was no answer. Did you know your front door was unlocked?"

Carol figured that she was so upset when she got home last night, that she forgot to lock it.

"Why did you come?" Carol asked weakly.

"That's not important now. Actually, I have a couple who want to see the house, but that will have to wait until you feel better. Try to eat some more."

With every bite, Carol felt like she was eating crow.

Wendy went out of the room and soon returned with a towel and a bucket.

"Here, in case anything comes up. Are you certain you don't want to go to the hospital? No. Is there anyone you want me to call? No. I hate to leave you. I have an appointment in an hour. I could cancel it if you'd like me to stay. No."

Carol shook her head until she was almost dizzy.

"I'll be right back, I just need to make a call," Wendy said, and she left the room.

How could she have been so quick to misjudge this woman, Carol thought. Was that someone else knocking on the door? She heard Wendy's voice, then the voice of a man. It was Mike. Wendy stepped into the bedroom.

"Are you well enough for a visitor?" Wendy asked, smiling. Before Carol could answer, Mike Jarmon came into the room. He regarded Carol with concern and pity.

He approached her bedside and asked if she was all right. She nodded unconvincingly.

Carol turned to Wendy and said, "This is like an open house."

Wendy laughed. "Just about. It looks like you're in good hands now, so I have to run. I'll call you later to see how you're doing." Wendy touched Carol's forehead.

Carol said, "Wendy, thank you." She felt like she was about to burst into tears.

"Oh, sweetie, you're welcome."

Wendy turned to Mike and gave him one of her business cards with a big smile. "Call me if you need anything. Anything at all."

Carol closed her eyes and shook her head. She almost felt like throwing up.

"I'll let myself out," Wendy said and gave a wave goodbye with her fingers.

Mike sat on the bed and regarded Carol with love and pity.

"I can't help but feel this is because of what I told you last night," he said, remorsefully. "Is it? You would have found out eventually. I'm sorry I'm the one who told you."

"No, no, no," Carol repeated. "Don't feel bad. It's just…" She didn't know how to finish that.

He looked at the dishes around the bed.

"Are you done with all this?" he asked.

She looked around at the food she had barely eaten and nodded.

"I'll clean this up." Mike felt her coffee cup. It was cold. "I'm going to make myself a coffee. Do you want another?"

She shook her head. Mike cleared the dishes and took them to the kitchen. Carol closed her eyes again and tried to sleep.

Something woke her. Was it a sound? A voice? What was it?

Carol stirred herself. She did not feel much better, and it was everything she could do to get out of bed. It was getting on towards evening by the look of the light coming into the house. Standing in the doorway of her bedroom she peered out cautiously. It was quiet. Looking toward the kitchen she could detect no sound or movement.

"Mike," she tried to call out, but her voice failed, and the name escaped as a weak utterance. She tried again only this time louder and clearer.

"In here," he said, and at the exact time he said it, Carol realized the craft room door was open. She was certain it had been locked. Wendy—Wendy must have opened it for some reason.

"Mike, don't go in that room! Mike!" Carol took quick steps to the craft room and stood in the doorway looking in.

Mike stood there looking at her. She did not like that look. The cross-stitch was in plain sight but what caused Carol's head to swim was the Smith Falls chart. Mike was holding it in his hands.

The two stood staring at each other. Carol could not say anything.

"Carol, what is this?" he asked her. His voice was a hoarse whisper, and there was accusation and subtle shock in his words. She did not answer him.

"Carol," he said more forcefully. "What is this?"

"What?"

"Don't give me what—this!" he said harshly, holding up the chart towards her face.

"It's my chart, my cross-stitch pattern," she said, trying to sound innocent.

"It's got a torn corner, like the corner piece we found in Tina DeLuca's hand!"

"So?"

"So! So! When we first met, I asked you to show me the chart of the cross-stitch you were working on the day Tina DeLuca was found. You showed me the one with flowers on it. What cross-stitch were you working on the day your group met at Tina's house?"

"I can't rightly remember. It may have been the flowers."

"Please, don't lie to me!"

Carol knew she was caught, yet she could not stop trying to get away like some animals when caught in a trap will chew off their leg to get free.

"Okay, okay. I might have been working on this one, but when you told me that Tina was found with a corner of my chart in her hands, I thought you might suspect me of something, so I lied."

"You lied?"

"Maybe the corner piece Tina had in her hand was from my chart—"

"Maybe?"

"Okay, it probably is, but it may have been accidentally torn off during our meeting and... and after I left Tina found it on the floor or in the cushion of the chair I was sitting in, and... and she was going to drop it in the garbage, but... but she slipped and fell before she did. That's why it was in her hand."

Mike stared at her in disbelief.

"Don't you believe me?" she asked, desperately.

"No!"

"But that is what happened."

He dropped the chart on her chair. "I have to go," he said.

Carol called his name all the way to the door. "Mike, where are you going? What are you going to do? Mike!"

He did not answer or look at her but stormed out.

Carol stood at the door and watched him drive off. Before she closed the door, she knew what she was going to do.

25

Carol found her phone and considered calling Harriet. Then she reconsidered and called Amanda. "Amanda, it's Carol."

Amanda was her usual upbeat self. "Oh, hi Carol, how are you?"

"To be honest, I'm not feeling that good. To be honest, I'm as sick as a dog and I need a favor."

"Sure, we just finished dinner. What do you need?"

"I'm not up to driving myself. I need you to drive me somewhere."

"Where, the hospital?"

"No, not the hospital."

"Then where?"

"I need you to drive me to a craft store."

Amanda was at Carol's house in fifteen minutes.

Carol was standing by her front door when she saw Amanda drive up. She got in the car. Amanda could see that Carol was ill. She looked pale and tired, while her eyes were red with dark circles underneath.

"Carol, are you okay?" Amanda said with justified concern.

"I'm not well enough to drive, but I can make the ride. Thanks for picking me up."

"To which craft store are we going?"

"Get on 101 South and it's passed Amherst."

They drove as the sun sank in the western sky.

"Carol, I think you should be in bed," Amanda said, as she kept her eyes on the road and her friend.

"I know, Amanda, but this is important."

"What could be so important that you need to go to this craft shop? What do you need so badly you would risk your health?"

"My health? I'm worried about my life."

"What is that supposed to mean?" Amanda turned to her.

"Eyes on the road, Amanda!"

The car was drifting over the centerline of the road.

If Carol thought it was difficult finding the craft store on her own, it was somehow worse with Amanda. Before dark, they found it.

"Do me a favor, Amanda," Carol said, before getting out of the car. "Please, stay in the car while I go in."

"Why can't I go in with you?" Amanda said, and she reminded Carol of a child.

"Please, Amanda, for your own safety's sake. I love you and I don't want anything to happen to you."

"Happen to me? What could possibly happen at a craft store?"

Carol reached over, put her hand on her friend's hand, and gave it a reassuring squeeze. "I'll be back in a few minutes. Please, wait here."

Getting out of the car, Carol went to the door. It was not yet dark, so the overhead light was not turned on. She tried the door. It was locked. She knocked. Carol looked through the glass on the door. She knocked again. No lights and no movement. Her heart sank. She wasn't exactly certain what she would gain by coming here again but she was hoping Agatha could help her somehow. Tina might die and Carol might be arrested by her boyfriend. Agatha had to have some answers.

She tried the door again and knocked loudly. No answer. Carol turned to Amanda who raised her hands, palms up, in exasperation. Carol looked around. Frustrated she began to walk back to the car.

"Yup."

The voice startled her. She turned and standing by the corner of the building was the creepy grave digger. He was dressed exactly the same as before. Did he carry that shovel with him everywhere, Carol wondered. She was not quite as afraid of him this time. Carol held her ground.

"Is the store closed today?" she asked.

"Yup. Closed today," he said, holding his ground as well.

"I wished to speak with Agatha. Is she about? Do you

know where I can find her?"

He nodded. "It is because of Agatha that the store is closed."

"Where is she? It is important I speak with her."

"They take her away."

"Away? Away where?"

"Doctors. Doctors take her to hospital."

"Is she sick?"

He nodded. "Cancer. Agatha has the cancer."

"Oh," Carol said, feebly. "I'm sorry."

"Agatha has always been sickly, even as a child," he said sadly. "Pity she got the cancer, atop the other thing. Some get more than their share of grief, I suppose."

"Other thing? What other thing?"

"You spoke with her, yes?"

"Yes."

"Then you must know what I'm talking about."

"But I don't."

"But you spoke to her. You must know."

"I don't know what you are talking about," Carol insisted.

"My sister, Agatha was never right in the head," he said, tapping the side of his head to signify mental illness.

"What?"

"She was known to say strange, even bizarre things. Sometimes she scared off customers with her crazy talk. One could never take what she said seriously."

"I don't believe it," she said, as if in a daze.

"If Agatha said anything to you that was out of line, well, then, I apologize. She never meant any harm. She's just, you know, sick in the head. Agatha isn't a bad person, mind you. She's just crazy."

Carol could only stare at the man in disbelief.

"What did you want to see Agatha about, anyway?" he asked.

Carol turned away from him and walked slowly back to Amanda's car as if in a daze. What was she to make of all this? She got in the car and did not answer one of Amanda's dozen questions.

"What do we do now, Carol?" was Amanda's last question.

Carol sat there feeling totally defeated. "I don't care. Let's go home."

Just then a tap on Carol's window made her jump. Agatha's brother had his face close to the window. He had said something Carol did not hear very well. She brought down the window about three inches.

"Is your name Carol?" he asked.

She was about to say no, not wanting him to know even that much, but she decided to be honest.

"Yes, my name is Carol."

"Funny thing happened when I was leaving Agatha's bedside in the hospital. She grabbed a hold of my arm and said, 'Tell Carol to finish the cross-stitch.' I didn't know what she meant by that exactly, but Agatha said it like it was very important. I just thought I'd tell you."

"Thank you," Carol said, raised the window, and told Amanda to drive.

Amanda waited until they were on the 101 before she asked, "What was that all about?"

"That is where I got the cross-stitch."

"Which cross-stitch?"

"The Smith Falls cross-stitch."

"I remember that. I thought you stopped working on it." When Carol did not respond, Amanda said, "Who is Agatha?"

"She is that guy's sister. Agatha is in the hospital with cancer. She was working in the store when I came and gave me the cross-stitch."

"Gave it to you? Sold it to you, you mean."

"Yes, I guess that is what I meant to say."

After a few more miles, Carol said, "Amanda, have you spoken with Vincent recently, about Tina's condition?"

"Yes, about five days ago. Still no change."

"I went to the hospital the other day—"

"I wished you had called me. I would have gone with you."

"When I was there, I happened to overhear two nurses talking about Tina. They used the term 'vegetative state'. I believe Tina is much worse off than we have been told."

"Why would Vincent lie about that?" Amanda asked angrily. "Carol, are you sure you heard right?"

Carol did not wish to tell Amanda that this information had come from Mike. Even though she might not see him again, she did not wish to get him into any trouble.

"I'm pretty sure I heard right. I'm telling you this because you're my friend and you have a right to know the truth. You care about Tina, we all do. I think you should tell Harriet and Margaret. I think Vincent plans on taking Tina off her machines."

"Carol, what are you saying? Vincent would never do that! I can't believe you're saying this!"

"All right, all right Amanda. Let's just forget it."

Neither of the women said anything more on the drive to Bedford.

By the time Amanda dropped Carol off at her house it was dark. Carol thanked Amanda and told her she would call her tomorrow. Amanda waited until Carol was in the house before she drove away.

For some strange reason, Carol felt light-headed. She was no longer sick, but this new feeling was surreal, almost dreamlike. It almost felt like she was on some drug. Carol did not know what to make of what Agatha's brother told her. It was not hard to believe that Agatha had cancer. She did not look at all healthy, but when the brother said that Agatha was mentally ill, that almost brought Carol's already crumbling world down on her head. Agatha is unbalanced, unhinged, demented, deranged crazy, cuckoo. Was everything Agatha said to Carol only the inane ramblings of a disturbed mind? Was Smith Falls just an induced psychosis Carol had somehow got from Agatha? Was Carol losing her mind as well? Did Carol simply create Smith Falls in her mind? How could that be?

Carol began to shake all over. Get a grip! Get a grip, she told herself. You're losing it. You're going to end up in the psych ward next to Agatha. This is impossible, she thought. How can this be happening? How can she ever trust her thoughts again? Carol felt she had lost her hold on reality. Please, let this not be true. Please, let this not be true. She had to sit down. Have a drink. No. No alcohol! She tried to think, but her thoughts ran around and around in a vicious circle that went nowhere. Is this what it is like to go insane?

What were Agatha's last words to her brother? 'Tell Carol to finish the cross-stitch.' Then that is exactly what Carol is going to do. Tonight. This very night that cross-stitch will be finished, and then we'll see!

26

Practically all the thread that came with the kit was used up. Miraculously, they had calculated the amount of thread needed to the inch. All that was left to do on Smith Falls was to finish the backstitching. Backstitching was indicated on the chart with an extra heavy line. It was a stitch that acted as an outline and added detail to items on the pattern. Backstitches are generally a darker color than the color of the pattern.

Carol lost count of how much coffee she had that night. She played no music. It was so quiet. Sometimes she would stop and listen, half expecting the sound of a storm with thunder and lightning, and great elemental forces converging to mark the portent of the coming of some great magic or mystical powers. But there was nothing. Nothing but calm.

Hour after hour Carol worked diligently, almost unceasingly. At regular intervals, she would stand and loosen up. She shook her hands so they would not cramp and stretch her wrists. A trip to the bathroom helped, but very soon she was right back at it.

There had never been a time when she worked on a pattern like this—these last few months had been a revelation, of sorts. Carol had learned a lot and one of those things she learned was what she was capable of doing regarding her cross-stitching. It was no longer a hobby or something to pass the time. Now it had purpose and meaning and fulfillment. She felt as if she were working for something bigger, something outside of herself or her selfishness. She had wanted this cross-stitch to use in a competition—a blue ribbon! That ribbon was petty and meaningless now. She was creating a doorway to another world, another life; a life where she could escape all the mistakes and consequences of this one. What was it that Janette Jarmon had said? It is a shame we cannot remove our mistakes in life as easily as we can remove mistakes from a cross-stitch. But that is what Carol believed she was doing. Smith Falls allowed her to remove or escape her mistakes in life. There was a brave new world awaiting her just beyond this cross-stitch, and she was eager to go there.

The backstitching took time. Never had she been more focused and more driven. Stitch after stitch she drew closer to completion. Stitch by stitch she was creating her destiny and sealing her fate. Carol realized she had finally made her choice.

Oh, my God, it is done! That is the last stitch. Practically all her floss was used up. She looked at her cross-stitch and sat in wonder at it. It was beautiful. Smith Falls was a work of art beyond anything she had previously created. It was difficult to think of it as only a cross-stitch, as it appeared to pulsate with life as if it were breathing. Glorious, she thought. The finished work was hypnotic. She could not stop looking at it. Carol felt happy and contented. She had finally created something worthwhile and beautiful. Tears welled in her eyes. This was a blue-ribbon winner. Think of the praise people would shower upon her, the sheer admiration she would garner if she were to enter it in a competition. But that would not happen. She had other plans for this cross-stitch.

Carol sat and waited. When would it happen, she wondered. When would she find herself in Smith Falls?

It was daylight. She had worked all through the night and most of the morning. Carol was tired, but it was a tired born from creating something wonderful. She continued to stare at the cross-stitch. When would it happen? Perhaps if she stared at it and concentrated on Smith Falls. Carol continued to stare at the place she knew so well—the bandstand, the shops, the horse and carriage, and the foliage. There was Penelope and Robert, walking down the street, and Mr. Walter Pennington was walking jauntily with his stick. She knew them all and loved them all. That is where she longed to be. Why was it not happening? What could she have forgotten? Carol looked at the instructions on the back of the chart. She read over each one carefully, marking off the ones she did correctly. Some had not been done quite correctly, she had to admit. Carol had shown the partly completed work to the members of her group, and even let the chart be taken by Tina, albeit temporarily, and part of the chart was torn off. Mike Jarmon had the torn piece, plus he had seen the chart and he most likely saw the almost completed Smith Falls. Did all these things create the reason she could not return there? Please, please, please, let it happen, she said to herself. She so desperately needed to escape. Mike had the torn piece of chart, she considered. Did she need to get it back? She didn't know. How could she get it back?

Carol continued reading the instructions and reread the detailed backstitching instructions. Below that was a line Carol could not recall seeing before.

After the backstitching is complete stitch your initials in the lower right-hand corner of the cross-stitch using two strands of the black floss.

How did she fail to see this before?

A heavy knock on the door gave her a start. What now?

Carol got up and going to the door she listened. Another knock. She went down the hall so she could see out the front window. That was Mike's car and there was a marked police car blocking her driveway.

"Carol, open up! It's Mike Jarmon! I have two police officers with me!"

Carol raced back to the room and locked the door. She frantically looked for her needle and the black floss. She cut a length and separated two strands. Threading the needle, she started to stitch her initials.

"Carol, are you home?" Mike's voice was clearer now. He was in the house. "You left your front door unlocked again. That's a bad habit. Carol, where are you? Carol, are you in there?"

He was just outside her craft room door. The doorknob jiggled.

"Carol, open the door!"

"All right, I'm coming. I'm coming out," she called as she stitched frantically.

"Carol, open the door right now. We must ask you some questions. I talked with Vincent DeLuca this morning. He told me some interesting things. Carol! Carol, open this door, or I'll force it open!"

"Coming!"

"Carol, I'm coming in!"

The interior door wasn't meant to be a great barrier. It was one of those light, hollow doors, and the locking mechanism was not particularly strong. Mike Jarmon put his shoulder to the door and with a bit of effort it sprang open.

He stepped into the room. There was no one in the room but himself. He stared open-mouthed.

"Carol!" He called out again. It was a small room. He gave it a quick look. Going to the door, he called out to the two officers—one female, one male. "You two, search the house! Check to see if she went out back."

Mike Jarmon turned back into the room. He searched the small closet—empty. He checked the one window—closed and locked on the inside. He was certain her voice came from this room. There was practically no place a woman could hide in here, he knew. He was about to search another room when something struck him. Something else was missing. He turned to the floor stand that had held Carol's cross-stitch when he was in the room previously. There was no cross-stitch in the frame. All her material—the different colored threads were gone. Even the torn pattern he'd seen that had brought this entire thing to a head; that too, was missing.

That morning Jarmon had gone to talk to Vincent DeLuca. When Mike started to build a case against him and threatened to hold up any euthanasia procedure on his wife, DeLuca began to tell all he knew. DeLuca spoke of the slippers and Carol going to Tina's room at the hospital, watching his house, and following him around in her car. DeLuca was very forthcoming in giving his theory that Carol may have had a hand in Tina's fateful fall.

Jarmon suspected as much, and so with two uniformed officers he went to Carol's house to bring her in for questioning. The question now was; where had Carol disappeared to?

Amanda called Harriet and tried to explain to her about taking Carol to the craft store, and the circumstances that surrounded it, including Carol's claim of Tina's true medical status and Vincent's intent to take Tina off her machine in the hospital.

Amanda was so excited and animated on the phone, she had a difficult time organizing her thoughts, causing her message to come off confusing and disjointed. Harriet thought it might be advantageous if she and Margaret came to Amanda's house where they could sit down calmly with a cup of tea and discuss the matter.

About an hour later Harriet and Margaret pulled up in

front of Amanda's house. Amanda had prepared for the ladies a light snack with their tea.

"Now, Amanda, as calmly and succinctly as possible tell us what happened," Harriet told her, in a very motherly manner.

"Yesterday, Carol called me and told me she was sick and asked me to drive her to a craft store. This was the craft store where she bought the Smith Falls cross-stitch. The store is past Amherst and in the country."

"What is the name of the store?" Margaret asked.

"I can't recall exactly. Mullins or Manells or something."

"Did Carol say why she needed to go there?" Harriet asked. "Didn't you say she was sick?

"Carol did not look good," Amanda said. "But she never told me why she needed to go there. Anyway, we got there but Carol found the store closed. The door was locked. Then this creepy guy carrying a shovel—"

"A shovel?" Harriet said, a bit shocked.

"Yes, he had a shovel. He and Carol talked a bit and Carol got in the car. Then the shovel guy came over to Carol's side and asked her if her name was Carol. She said yes and he said his sister, Agatha, had a message for her. Carol was to finish her cross-stitch."

"Her cross-stitch?" Harriet repeated. "What cross-stitch?"

"Smith Falls, I suppose. Carol said she got it at that store."

"What else did Carol say?"

"That the woman who runs the store, the shovel guy's sister, is in the hospital with cancer."

The three women sat silently thinking of what all this could mean.

"Now what was this thing Carol said about Tina and Vincent?"

"Carol said that she overheard that Tina was not doing well at all. Tina is not simply in a coma, but she is actually in a vegetative state."

"Vegetative state," Margaret said. "That is very serious."

"Meanwhile Vincent has been telling me that Tina is in a coma and there has been no change in her condition. Then Carol drops a bomb. She said that Vincent had been talking about euthanasia—ending Tina's life."

"Where did Carol hear all this?" Harriet wanted to know.

"Carol said she was at the hospital and overheard nurses talking about it."

"We should try to contact Vincent and ask him directly," Margaret said.

Amanda called Vincent right away but could not get through.

"What do we do now?" Amanda asked.

"Now," Harriet said, "would be a good time to pray."

Amanda's phone rang. She answered it.

"Hello, is this Amanda Simons?"

"Yes, this is Amanda."

"Amanda, I don't know if you remember me. This is Det. Mike Jarmon. We spoke months ago about Tina DeLuca."

Amanda made a shocked face to her friends, then put her phone on speaker so the other women could hear.

"Oh, yes, Det. Jarmon, I remember you."

Harriet raised her hand to her mouth wondering why he was phoning.

"Listen, Amanda, I need to know if you have heard from your friend Carol Crane."

"Carol? I heard from her yesterday. She told me she was feeling sickly."

"Was that morning or evening or what?"

"It was getting on toward evening."

"You haven't heard from her today?"

"No."

"Do you have any idea where she might be?"

"No."

"Do you think the other members of your cross-stitch group might know where Carol is?"

"They are both right here with me. You could ask them. I have you on speaker."

Jarmon was surprised at this and proceeded to ask Margaret and Harriet. They naturally admitted they had not spoken with Carol lately and had no idea where she could be.

"Have you tried contacting Carol's ex-husband?" Harriet asked.

"Yes, I have. Mr. Crane has not heard or seen her in over a week."

"Det. Jarmon," Harriet spoke, "What is all this about? Why are you looking for Carol?"

There was a long pause. "I cannot find her anywhere, and I desperately need to get in touch with her."

"You tried her house, of course," Harriet said.

"Yes, I tried her house, and she isn't home."

"Well, if any of us hear from Carol, we will certainly let you know," Harriet said.

"Thank you, ladies. Goodbye."

Amanda hung up her phone and they all looked at one another.

"Now what was that all about?" Harriet asked.

Mike Jarmon stood in the craft room in Carol's house. He wondered if those women were being honest with them. Did they know what he knew about Carol? Did they know where she was? Carol could have been in the room with them. Mike walked through the house. The other officers had been dismissed and he was alone in the house. He had a hard time leaving the house not knowing how Carol got out without being seen. She had to have been in the room. He knew her voice on the other side of that door. There was no clever recording device like in a cheap novel, and even if there were, where was it? He had found no speaker or hose or anything to emit her voice. She had been in that room and then in an instant, she wasn't. Mike did not know how he was going to write his report.

Vincent DeLuca stood by his wife's bedside. Tina's accident had been a horrific ordeal from the day he had discovered her unconscious and bleeding on their floor, then her prognosis that she would never recover, until now when he had to make that heart-rending decision to end her life. Even early on when the doctors told Vincent that Tina would not recover, he did not give up hoping some miracle would bring her back. He waited and waited. Maybe God was punishing him for his sins. He had always loved Tina, and he still did. Why did he carry on with other women? What drove him to do it? He wished he knew. He wished things had never come to this.

His phone vibrated. Vincent looked at the Caller ID. Amanda again. He would have to block her calls. He was not inclined to answer any more of her questions. As far as he was concerned, those cross-stitchers were not a part of his life, and he owed them no explanation.

Vincent wondered if the information he gave that police detective was going to lead to anything.

27

Amanda was trying not to be frustrated, but she was finding it difficult to stay calm. She had Harriet and Margaret in the car, and adding to her exasperation was the strong possibility that she was lost.

"I was certain that Carol and I came this way," Amanda uttered. "It has to be around here somewhere."

"Didn't you write down the address?" asked Harriet from the passenger seat.

"No Harriet, I didn't."

"I think we're lost," Margaret spoke from the rear seat.

"Thank you, Margaret, I know we're lost," Amanda said.

"What is the name of the place?" asked Harriet.

"I don't know."

"But you were there, weren't you?" said Margaret.

"Yes, Margaret, I was there—once."

"Better pull into this service station and ask for directions," Harriet said.

Amanda pulled into the small service station. It had only two pumps, a small garage, and a store. The car ran over the signal bell hose and the station attendant came out. He was a slow-walking middle-aged, thin man who continually wiped his hands with a rag.

"Fill 'er up?" he asked.

"We're looking for a place," Amanda said to the man who stood by the side of the car. "It's a store, a craft store. I don't know the name of it, but it's supposed to be around here somewhere."

"A craft store," he repeated. "That sounds familiar."

"Do you know where it is?" Harriet said, leaning over so she could see him.

He looked up and down the road, then looked at the women in the car and said, "No, I don't have a clue where that place is."

"Thank you," they all called out, their voices tinged with disappointment.

After driving for about an hour Amanda exclaimed, "There it is! I knew we'd find it. Malum Crafts."

"This is the place Carol said she got her cross-stitch—Smith Falls?" Margaret asked.

"Yes, this is the place," Amanda said, taking in the store and the surroundings.

"What's wrong, Margaret?" Harriet said, looking at the back seat. "You don't look very good."

Margaret leaned forward and touched Amanda on the shoulder.

"Amanda, turn the car around and drive us home. Hurry! Do it now! Drive!"

There was such urgency in Margaret's voice that Amanda turned to Harriet for directions on what to do.

Harriet studied Margaret's face. She remembered Margaret looking like that once before, but this time was more intense.

"You better do as she says, Amanda," Harriet said, looking at the store, then back at Margaret. "Drive! Get us out of here! Now!"

Amanda backed up the car, turned onto the road, and drove fast.

None of them said a word on the drive back to Bedford. Amanda dropped the other two off at Margaret's apartment building. Harriet had driven there so Amanda would only have to stop once to pick them up. Amanda had told them about her trip with Carol out to the craft store. Now that Carol was missing, they all thought they might learn something since Carol was intent on going there even though she was ill. Unfortunately, Amanda could not remember the exact location or name of the craft store. They had to drive around for miles looking for it. They finally found it only to have Margaret insist they return home. Amanda was so frustrated she let her friends off and went home.

Harriet went up with Margaret to her apartment. Harriet had some questions for her friend. Neither spoke a word until they got inside the apartment. Once the door was closed, Margaret asked Harriet if she wanted a cup of tea. Harriet said yes.

The two women sat in Margaret's small living room sipping their tea.

"Margaret, do you want to tell me what that was all about?" Harriet said.

Margaret looked at her questioningly, as if she did not know to what Harriet referred.

"Why did you insist on leaving as soon as we got to the craft store?"

Margaret turned away. There was a frightened look on her face. She bit her upper lip.

"I got a very strange feel off that place," Margaret said. She spoke quietly as if she did not want anyone to hear.

Harriet thought this was peculiar since they were alone and no one else was in the room.

"What kind of feeling?" Harriet asked, but she was afraid she knew the answer.

"There is something terribly wrong with that place," Margaret said. "I sensed... evil. Even the name of the place, Malum Crafts—Malum is Latin, it means evil. I should have known sooner. When I first saw Carol's new cross-stitch— you know, Smith Falls—I sensed something off it. It was not good."

"What do you think happened to Carol?" Harriet asked.

Margaret shook her head. "Whatever happened was not natural—not... Godly."

The two women sat in silence for several minutes.

"Not much of a group now," Harriet said. "We lost Tina, and God knows what's become of Carol."

"Poor Tina," Margaret said. "Has it been a week?"

"Nine days," said Harriet. "That Vincent did everything so private. We don't even know where Tina is buried. Now, it's just the three of us."

"I don't think Det. Jarmon will let his mother join our group," Margaret added. "Too bad, she sounded like a nice woman."

28

Everyone in Smith Falls always looked forward to one of Lady Wyndemere's Balls. It was the highlight of the season and a very good reason to use the ballroom in her home, which usually stood empty the rest of the year. Guests began to arrive at the Wyndemere estate at about nine in the evening. Most guests arrived in fine coaches; a light two-passenger enclosed brougham, a four-passenger landau with a retractable roof, a four-wheeled barouche, or a surrey with a fringe canopy. One could even see an elegant clarence with a projecting glass front.

The Wyndemere mansion was a tall square structure with tall pillars out front. Between the pillars, wide double doors stood open for guests. The doors opened into a great hall with a black and white square tile floor. Directly across the great hall was an arched opening that led to the ballroom. The ballroom was lit by numerous chandeliers each holding scores of lighted candles. There were also candle sticks, candelabras, decorative oil-filled hurricane lamps, and gas wall sconces. Adorning the room were arbors trimmed with wisteria vines. Tall vases set in floor stands were filled to overflowing with flowers—roses, carnations, peonies, and hydrangeas. The ballroom was two stories high, and the floor was of dark hardwood. At one end of the ballroom, high above the dance floor, was a balustraded terrace for the orchestra. Garlands of eucalyptus and white roses hung from the balustrades.

Everyone who attended the ball was dressed in their best formal wear. The men at the ball were all dressed in black tuxedos with either a V-shaped or a U-shaped silk vest. Men's vests had two small pockets, one for a watch and chain. Some tuxedos had satin lapels, and in their left lapel, every man wore a boutonniere. Beneath they wore white shirts with a high collar and a white bowtie. They all looked quite dashing, and most men looked quite similar in their dress. The same could not be said for the women whose gowns differed in color and style.

The women were all in floor-length gowns replete with ornamentations of frills, lace, buttons, bows, beads of gold, silver, and crystal, and metallic embroideries of silk cords. Some necklines, especially on younger women hung for their shoulders, and gloves covering from their fingertips to their elbows. Some gowns were vibrantly colored, some multicolored, some white, some pearl, some eggshell. Plum and navy blue were popular colors. Most gowns had lavishly designed surfaces trimmed with ribbons, rosettes, and lace. If all the men looked dashing, then all the women looked enchanting.

There must have been one hundred and fifty guests and some of them Carol had met at the garden party. Guests milled about going from one group to another and joining in conversations. Introductions were made, and old friendships were renewed. At one point Lady Wyndemere appeared above in front of the orchestra and looking down she welcomed her guests.

"My friends, I would like to formally welcome you all to Wyndemere Estate," she said. "Thank you all for coming and for helping to make this night a festive and memorable event. Just so you know, anyone who does not have a good time will not be invited back." There was laughter from everyone. "In the adjoining rooms are refreshments and dinner will be served at midnight. Just a word of warning to the more … let us say, the more enthusiastic. No one should be on the property after 4:00 a.m. I hope that is understood. Now, we will begin festivities with The Grand March." She turned to the orchestra and indicated they commenced with the music.

The Grand March, Carol was to learn, began with a single couple marching around the room, picking up other couples behind them in tow. When everyone was marching the lead couple came down the middle of the room and reaching the end, couples broke off going left and right and marched off to the rear. At the rear of the room the lead couples from the left and right link up creating a line of four. This was repeated until lines of couples the width of the room ended up in rows of couples all linking arms and facing forward.

It was an enjoyable communal dance that required little skill. Carol, who never participated in a Grand March, simply took her lead from Walter Pennington. At the end, everyone applauded.

Guests were given a brief respite before the next dance which was a quadrille where four couples danced in a rectangular formation. Not everyone danced the quadrille, as some were content with watching. The dance reminded

Carol of square dancing in which she and Gary had a brief interest years ago. She and Walter paired with Penelope and Robert and two other couples. They danced The Star, The Visits and The Cotilion. The was a lot of turning, parading, coming together and apart. There was a good deal of clasping and unclasping hands with members of her group. Carol found if she watched the other women and their moves, and she trusted her partner she got through the dance like she was bred to it. It was the most fun she ever had.

There was another break and Walter asked Carol if she wished for a refreshment.

"I do indeed," she said realizing she was now parched.

Walter escorted her to one of the side rooms where a punch bowl was set up. Like the punch at the garden party, Carol found it intoxicating. But she had to admit the entire evening was quite exhilarating.

"Are you enjoying yourself?" Walter asked her.

"I truly am," she said. "I am so glad to be here with you."

"So am I," he said.

Penelope and Robert joined them for a drink.

"How did you like the dance, Caroline?" Penelope asked.

"I liked it very much."

"I did not know you were such a good dancer."

"Thank you, Penelope. I did not know I was a good dancer either," Carol said, and they all laughed.

"I have to say, Caroline," said Robert, "that you are the second most beautiful woman here."

"I was just going to tell Penelope the same thing," said Walter with a grin.

Each dance brought on a new sensation, and particularly for Carol, a new experience and each stimulated her senses. At first, Carol was hesitant that she would be like a fish out of water at the ball but soon discovered that she instinctually knew what to do, how to act, and what to say. This is my home now, she realized. I am never going back. Carol had made her decision and she accepted it fully. She would soon forget her other life and adapt to this one.

It was now after 11:00 and the next dance was a waltz. Compared to the other dances the waltz was one of raving rapidity in which partners held on to one another firmly as they spun repeatedly and circled about the room. Carol grew dizzy and giddy from the repetitive motion, and it somehow activated a pleasure principle within her. It was a psychic force that could only be satisfied with more of the same. It was a dance that suited Carol for it reflected her mystifying escape to a fantasy life that so differed from her previous existence. The repetitive motion of the dance was hypnotic and addictive.

When it was done, overpowering light-headedness plagued her, and she gasped for breath.

Walter regarded her closely. "Caroline, are you feeling well?" he asked concerned.

She nodded. "It was simply so exhilarating."

He took her by the arm. "Here, let's get you some fresh air." Walter led Carol through some rooms until they came to a stone patio. "Breathe deep," he said.

She did so, but the fresh air seemed to intoxicate her even more.

"Would you like me to get you a drink of water?" he asked.

She nodded trying to catch her breath. "Perhaps that would be wise."

Walter looked around and sat her on the stone rail that ran around the patio.

"Stay right here, and I will be right back," he said.

"I'm not leaving," she said smiling.

Carol looked up at the stars. Never had she beheld stars so bright. It was a beautiful night. She feared to think that this was all a dream, and it would end.

A man approached from inside the house. The man was silhouetted in the door and from his dress it looked like Walter, but she knew it was too soon for him to have returned. The man approached her, and Carol recognized him as Rupert Collins, whom she had been introduced to this very evening.

"What are you doing out here all alone," Rupert said to her. His words were a bit slurred.

"I was feeling a bit dizzy, and Mr. Walter Pennington has gone to fetch me some water," she said.

"I was hoping to get a dance with you."

"Not this very moment," she said, laying her fingertips upon her forehead.

"Shall we just sit here together, we two?"

"Certainly, if you would like to wait with me until Mr. Walter Pennington returns."

"I'm certain old Walter wouldn't mind. Me and him are chuckaboos."

Just as she said it, Walter arrived carrying a glass of water. He handed it to Carol and watched her drink it. Walter turned to Rupert Collins.

"What's this, Rupert?" Walter said. "Come to steal a kiss from Miss Caroline, have you?"

"Come to steal a dance, old man," Rupert said.

"Not right this minute, Rupert, perhaps later," Walter said, tapping Rupert on the breast with the back of his hand. Walter felt something hard beneath Rupert's jacket. "What's this? What's this?" Walter said and quickly reaching inside Rupert's jacket, he extracted something from the man's breast pocket. It was a pewter flask.

"Rupert, have you been drinking," Walter said, leaning toward his friend and sniffing his breath. "Rupert, I believe you're a bit blinkered. I better keep this, and hope Lady Wyndemere does not find out that you brought spirits to her ball. Now, run along, Rupert, it appears I cannot trust you around my fiancé."

"Your what?" both Carol and Rupert exclaimed together.

"Now Rupert, see what you've done," Walter said with mock disappointment. "You've ruined Miss Caroline's surprise. Skidaddle out of here, Rupert, before I sit you down on the seat of your trousers."

Rupert Collins turned and walked away dejected with his head hanging low and his hands thrust into his trouser pockets.

Carol turned to Walter. "What was that you said?"

"What? Oh, you mean you being my fiancé. I did not mean for it to slip out like that. Here, allow me to get down on one knee." He did so, and taking her hands in his, Walter took on a more serious tone. "Caroline, I love you and I wish to marry you. Caroline, Caroline, say you'll be mine."

If Carol thought the waltz was dizzying, Walter's proposal almost caused her to faint. Fortunately, she was sitting at the time, and he was holding her hands in his to keep her from falling over. Walter stood at her side and gave her another drink of water. She drank some of the water and looked lovingly into his eyes. He was sitting on the cement rail next to her now, with one arm holding her. She could see he cared for her deeply, and she knew that she was in love with him. She nodded and said yes. He brought his face close to hers and kissed her passionately under the stars that were as eternal as love.

"I'm certain Penelope will love to hear this," Carol said, after a time.

"Oh, please, do not tell Penelope," he said, with a grin. "Telling Penelope would be like broadcasting it to the world. I must speak to Lady Wyndemere about this. I am certain she will want to have an engagement party for us before the year is out."

She took a long meaningful look at him. "Have I told you tonight how handsome you look?"

"I had to look my best, seeing I was escorting the most beautiful woman at the ball."

At midnight, dinner was served in a large room adjoining the ballroom. Tables had been set up laden with food. No one sat, as it was buffet style, but the tables were elegant with the best china, cutlery, and crystal. There was cold beef, ham, chicken, and duck, there were chicken croquettes, and chicken salad au celery. There was terrapin, salmon, and fried oysters. There were sandwiches, sweetbreads, clear soups, cheese, fruits, and vegetables. There were glasses of wines, champagne, and cups of coffee and tea. For dessert were dishes of sweet puddings and a variety of ices.

Carol was still reeling from Walter's proposal, and she did not have much of an appetite, but she ate to keep up her strength, for there was still much of the gala left.

Penelope drew Carol aside to speak in private.

"Caroline, you look like a girl who has a secret inside her just waiting to come out."

Carol shook her head as if not knowing to what Penelope referred.

"And I think I know what that secret is," Penelope said with a big smile.

"Oh, Penelope, promise me you won't tell anyone what you think my secret is. Promise me."

"All right, dear, I promise I will not say a word to anyone. Not even Robert."

The two women embraced.

"I am so very happy for you, dear Caroline," Penelope said.

After dinner the dancing resumed with a march in file which began with couples marching in single file hand-in-hand, then coming apart, circling, then coming together with the lead couple forming an arch and the other couple passing under. It was a good dance to ease into after the meal.

Carol was standing off to the side with Walter, Penelope, and Robert. The four of them were engaged in conversation while watching the dancers on the floor. Suddenly, to Carol's utter surprise, she saw a tall, dark-haired woman dancing. The woman was the spitting image of Tina DeLuca! She did not simply look like Tina; Carol knew it was Tina.

Carol felt stunned. She did not hear anything her companions said to her. She was barely aware of her surroundings. All she saw was this woman. How could Tina be here? How was it possible that she crossed over into Smith Falls? Then Carol remembered what Mike Jarmon had said about Vincent asking around the hospital about euthanasia. He must have done it. Vincent pulled the plug on Tina and now she was dead. But she wasn't dead! She was right here in Smith Falls at the ball. All of Carol's dreams of a perfect life in Smith Falls seemed to crash down on her head.

The dance ended and the man who had danced with Tina had her by the arm and escorted her over to Carol and her friends. Carol was familiar with the man. They had been introduced earlier in the evening. His name was Clive Toomy.

Toomy approached them with a smile and his right hand out. He shook hands with Walter and Robert and acknowledged Penelope and Carol.

"I wish you all to meet my dancing partner, Miss Christina," Clive Toomy said graciously. "She arrived late to the ball, and we have been making up for her tardiness." He turned to Tina and made the introductions. Tina wore a lovely gown that displayed her figure. Her dark hair was piled high making her look taller than she was. Around her neck, she wore a striking amethyst necklace with matching earrings. She looked quite lovely.

Tina greeted everyone in turn, but when she faced Carol, she said, "Surely we have already met."

"No, I do not believe so," said Carol.

Tina shook her head showing both recognition and confusion.

"We have met previously," Tina said. "I know I will remember in time."

"I saw her standing alone by the door, and I went right up to her, introduced myself, and asked her to dance," Clive Toomy said as if he could not believe his good fortune.

"Christina, I am certain we will get along famously," Penelope said. "Your dress is lovely."

Christina thanked her for the compliment.

The three men excused themselves and went to get their escorts a drink. Penelope turned to speak with someone else, leaving Carol and Tina looking at one another.

Tina said, "You know, Caroline, I am new to Smith Falls and I believe you have not been here very long as well. Do you know what we should do, Caroline, you and I? We should get some other women together and form a sewing circle."

The two women regarded each other closely.

Tina's appearance in Smith Falls could change everything for Carol. If Tina were to ever recall her other life and how Carol had caused her accident, she could reveal Carol's terrible secret, and the residents of Smith Falls would know what type of woman she was. Her new friends would reject her and surely Walter Pennington would retract his offer of marriage. Even if he did not, Lady Wyndemere would never let him marry someone like Carol. Maybe Walter would end up marrying Tina. Tina would marry Walter and Carol would be an outcast.

It was at that very instant Carol knew she would have to do something about Tina.

29

A few weeks later Amanda was on the road looking for Malum Crafts, except this time she was alone. She had promised Harriet she would never go back, but it all seemed ridiculous. Harriet had never even told her why she shouldn't go back. Amanda figured it had been something Margaret told Harriet. What it could be, Amanda didn't know. Margaret refused to talk to her about it.

So much had happened since Tina's death. Carol had gone missing without a trace. Det. Jarmon had suspected Gary of killing Carol, but there was no evidence. Margaret said that Gary didn't do it, though how Margaret would know that Amanda couldn't figure it out. Carol's cross-stitch of Smith

Falls was never found either. Now, that was strange. Who would take a cross-stitch? It was exceptional, though. Amanda couldn't imagine anyone taking Carol's cross-stitch, but stranger things than that have happened, though not many.

Amanda was not even certain she wanted to remain in the cross-stitch group. With Tina and Carol gone, there were now only the three of them. Harriet and Margaret seemed tight, and Amanda no longer felt she fit in with the older women. Maybe Amanda could start a new group with younger women like herself.

Amanda finally found Malum Crafts. She wondered how much business they would get out here in the boonies. The place looked old. She looked around to see if the brother was there.

No one appeared to be about the place. Amanda got out of the car and approached the door of the store. The doorknob turned and she pushed the door open. A shop bell rang over her head.

She stood still to see if the bell brought someone. The place seemed empty. Amanda slowly walked through the store looking over the inventory. At first glance, it looked very much like other craft stores, but it wasn't. There was a different feeling in this one, something she could not put her finger on or describe. Amanda strolled the aisles and still, she saw no one. She entered a part of the store where the walls rose high, and up on the wall were framed finished cross-stitches. But these cross-stitches were different than any she had ever seen. These were splendid, eye-catching, and unique. No, not all of them were different than any she had ever seen, for there at the end was one of an old town, Smith Falls. Surely this was the same one Carol had once worked on. In the center of the cross-stitch was a bandstand, and surrounding the bandstand was the small town of Smith Falls. Amanda looked at the characters walking the streets. One young couple was walking arm-in-arm, the woman was blonde and wore a long electric blue dress and a matching cape. A bonnet sat on one side of her head, and she carried a parasol. The woman's escort was dressed in a grey high hat with a brown band and long coat indicative of the times.

The quality and stitching gave the characters an incredibly life-like appearance.

There was one other couple on the cross-stitch. He was dressed similarly to the other man, save that this one carried a walking stick. On his arm, was a young lady with dark hair, dressed in a light blue dress with beaded stripes. She too wore a bonnet, and gloves, and carried a parasol.

But what shocked Amanda most was that this woman closely resembled Carol Crane. Amanda continued to study every detail of the cross-stitch. She saw in the lower right-hand corner two initials; C. C. Amanda was certain this was Carol's cross-stitch. She wished she could take down the cross-stitch to get a better look. So engrossed was she by the picture she did not realize a figure stood very close to her.

"Can I help you?"

The words startled Amanda who gasped. She wanted to scream but the sound came out in a gasp. She turned to see Agatha standing near her.

"I didn't know you were there," Amanda said, her hand pressed over her heart. "You startled me."

"Can I help you with something?"

Amanda looked at the strange woman. "Is your name Agatha?" she asked.

The woman nodded slightly.

"My friend and I were here weeks ago, and we spoke to your brother. He told us you were in the hospital. You're better now? I mean, you're here so you must be better now?"

Agatha did not respond with a word or a look. To Amanda it was unnerving.

"These cross-stitches on the wall are very... unique, aren't they? I've never seen any like that." Amanda said. "I have a friend who was working on this one—Smith Falls."

"Those cross-stitches are one-of-a-kind," Agatha said blandly. "We are the only store that carries them."

"One-of-a-kind?" Amanda repeated. "So that means this is the one my friend was working on? Did Carol give it to you?"

"It simply came back to us when she had finished it."

Amanda did not understand.

"The strange thing is my friend has gone missing. No one knows where she is. You must have read about it or seen it on the news. Her name is Carol Crane. Do you have any idea where she is?"

Agatha did not answer. Poor thing, thought Amanda, she must still be weak from cancer or the treatment. The woman appeared weak, and she moved and spoke slowly. Her dark eyes were heavy-lidded and dark circles appeared under them.

"Do you enjoy cross-stitch?" Agatha asked as she walked to the counter near the front of the store.

Amanda followed her. "Cross-stitch? Yes, I like it very much."

Agatha reached under the counter and said, "I have something here in which you might be interested."

Author's Note

If you got this far, then that means you finished the book, and I truly hope you enjoyed it. It is difficult to know exactly how I came to write this book. I think many authors would admit that a story often starts with a spark of an idea, and then takes on a life of its own. I cannot tell you what one book inspired me to write *The Enchanted Cross-Stitch*, though I would not be surprised if someone writes to me and tells me that my story reminds them of some other book.

If you like my book, I would appreciate it if you could recommend it to a friend.

The characters in my story are very real to me, and I feel like I know them, and to a degree, I care about them. The characters in *The Enchanted Cross-Stitch* are not based on individual people I know, but rather on types of people I have encountered in my life.

Some readers may be interested to know that I am currently working on my second book, which I plan to have published one way or another.

Christine Holly

Made in United States
North Haven, CT
04 May 2024

52104303R00129